House on Fire

a novel by
Carol Brisebois

Copyright © 2013 by Carol Brisebois
First Edition – January 2013

ISBN
978-1-4602-1164-9 (Paperback)

All rights reserved.

The characters and events in this book are fictitious. Similarities to real persons are coincidental and not intended by the author.

No part of this publication may be reproduced in any form, or by any means, electronic or mechanical, including photocopying, recording, or any information browsing, storage, or retrieval system, without permission in writing from the publisher.

Produced by:

FriesenPress
Suite 300 – 852 Fort Street
Victoria, BC, Canada V8W 1H8

www.friesenpress.com

Distributed to the trade by The Ingram Book Company

A heartfelt thank-you to my readers

This story is dedicated to you

"Ladybird, Ladybird, fly away home,
Your house is on Fire,
Your children shall burn!"
Mother Goose

one

Michael holed himself in his room and cranked the window shut. He slipped into the chair attached to the wooden school desk that belonged to another boy long ago. Drops of sweat crawled down his face and burned his cheeks.

He picked up a fat pencil laying in the desktop groove and suspended it over a blank sheet of paper. The picture trapped in his head hurt his eyes and refused to draw itself.

A regular kid wouldn't be inside on a summer afternoon. He'd be outside until his mommy called him for supper. The thick soles of his feet to protect him from the playground's stinging thistles, he'd chase away its bully, then celebrate his victory by climbing ten feet up the swing set and making dares to jump and be counted. Like the grandpa he never knew, but whose names he shared.

Michael. Frederick. Ballantine. With three weeks to go before grade one, he could print the first, second, and last. Tongue fixed to the corner of his mouth, he added his left-hand signature to the top of the page. His eyes scanned his work, and he frowned. Each letter E stood backwards, but he didn't know how to turn them over. Under his names, he drew a square box topped by a triangle that didn't look like his house. Adding a slanted chimney didn't help.

On both sides of the paper, the pencil scratched two batches of zigzags propped up by long lines. A smile crept around in Michael. These trees existed in his mind but not his front yard.

Linda popped open the door, and he startled.

She giggled. "Mommy says come to the table. Finish your picture later." She turned away, and, leaving the door open, headed into the hall.

He watched her brown curls bounce as she walked toward the kitchen. Fingers spread wide, he dropped the pencil to the desk. With the same hand, he crumpled the drawing and swatted it to the floor.

"What were you doing in your room?" Mommy sat across from him at the kitchen table. Beginning with Daddy's, she tonged spaghetti on the dinner plates, serving herself last. Her eyes flitted from one thing to the next the way small white butterflies do. "You were so quiet, I thought you'd gone to the park without telling me."

Long strands of pasta swung from Michael's mouth. He wrinkled his nose and looked up. Of all the mommies, she'd win the longest eyelashes contest. To marry a perfect lady like Daddy's would make one dream true. To become a man like him would make two.

Michael pictured James Ballantine standing at the Constructo Housing work-site. A Lucky Strike cigarette bounced between his lips. Others were tucked inside the black and silver striped case held by his shirt pocket, a present from Mommy. It had a built-in lighter he fired with a roll of his thumb, and, but for the jeweler's mistake, would have his initials. Instead of JFB, the engraving read DFB. Daddy said that made it more special.

Mommy didn't need lighters or fire or smoke. She chewed Wrigley's Doublemint gum. Linda put on her sweet voice and looked to her. "Janey wants me to meet her in the park after supper."

"Once the dishes are done." His mommy pushed herself away from the table, the chair's steel legs scraping the floor. "I have a treat." She picked up a package from the countertop, skated to the fridge, and grabbed a brick of ice cream.

"It's not from scratch, but IGA bakes a good pie." She sliced four pieces, and laid a frozen ball beside each.

Forks clinked rhythmically against plates, then stopped simultaneously as though on cue. Michael was asked to clear the table. After he stacked the dishes in the sink he was free to play in the square-shaped park behind the backyard fence.

Darren would be out there tonight. Sometimes he was a friend to Michael, but he did bad things too, like trample flowers, and pee on fire hydrants.

Michael decided not to risk the sky's hazy blue and stayed inside to play. Though his room got scary after the sun set. The imaginary enemies made him shake like a sparrow hiding among the pine tree branches. They chattered under his bed for hours. He tangled himself in his sheets, wondering how their voices would sound to others. If he fell asleep, they showed up in his dreams.

Michael closed the bedroom door behind him and set out on his idea to build a perfect home. He emptied the tube of Lincoln Logs on the floor. A lot of the wooden interlocking pieces were missing. Some had chipped ends, but these supplies were all he had.

He pressed together four log-cabin squares, making one room each for himself, his sister, and his parents, plus a bathroom. Shoving two more squares against those made a kitchen and a living room. He connected the logs one row on top of another, and tilted his head at the height of the walls.

A roof should be pointy, but the logs tumbled each time he tried to arrange them. He picked up two pieces of paper, and placed them on top at opposing angles. They refused to listen. Michael lay both flat and paused to consider his work. A house without windows or doors wouldn't let people look outside. A family trapped inside couldn't be happy.

He knocked the log structure to the hardwood and kicked every piece it was made of, along with the tube they came, in under his bed. His feet shoved the drawing on the floor there too. Soon his mommy would ask for his shorts and shirt. She'd make him wear his rocket-ship pyjamas.

They knelt beside each other. He recited the prayer. "Now I lay me down to sleep. I pray the Lord my soul to keep. If I should die before I wake, I pray the Lord my soul to take. Amen." The words prickled into his folded hands, but his mommy's face said she liked them. He didn't want to hurt her feelings. She was beautiful. And beautiful ladies cry easily.

~

"Look up. Look waaaaay up." The black and white man on the television screen stretched the word while the camera traveled from his knee-high boots to his face. Michael never saw a real giant, but this one would protect him, as kind as he was big.

"Are you ready?" The Friendly Giant said the same thing at the start of each show before he opened the drawbridge.

A castle would be a great place to live, but wouldn't fit in Michael's neighbourhood. There'd be nowhere for Daddy to park the car or Mommy to plant a garden. The moat surrounding it would have a no swimming sign.

If only he could remember all the rules and not just the loudest. Look both ways before you cross the street. Don't stick your tongue on a frozen fence. Keep forks out of sockets. Don't play with matches. There were more, but whether any stuck in Darren's head at all, he couldn't say. Though he was three years older, Darren had a hard time following them.

The two boys sat side by side in front of the television watching Rusty the Rooster and Jerome the Giraffe bob their puppet heads. They sang about games children play with windows. The Friendly Giant tapped his finger like a drumstick keeping time on the castle's window ledge.

Darren did his best to coax Michael away from the show and Mommy. Michael didn't like him, but that didn't mean he hated him. He guessed that being nice was one of the rules Darren's parents forgot to teach him. Michael knew a little about that family. Sometimes Darren shared secrets.

The first is that when it's time for trick or treating, he hides with his brothers and sisters in their basement. They wait for the kids outside to stop calling Halloween Apples before the lights go on again. And Darren's daddy has a projector he uses to watch movies about an angry man with a little mustache.

The worst secret Michael keeps for Darren is that he steals matches. Michael sees him play with them. This summer the two of them hid behind old Mr. Duncanson's shed six times when he was out buying groceries or walking his dog. Together they watched crumpled pages of the *Winnipeg Free Press* disappear.

A fire starts with kindling, bits of dry twigs and leaves. Darren showed him how to arrange them like a mouse-size teepee, leaving space for the flame. One balled-up page at a time makes it grow. Two feet stamp the fire to death before it gets so big someone catches you.

Darren has told Michael to strike the cardboard matchstick's red head, but he always refuses. Michael's stomach cracks like eggshells over what he knows.

After Mr. Friendly closes the drawbridge and the black and white cow jumps over the paper moon, Mommy switches off the television. Darren wants to ride bicycles in the grassy park. Michael follows Darren's silver fender with the red stripe running down the middle. They laugh when their tires bumpity-bump over the small hills near the sandbox.

~

That September morning the sun shone like it was another summer day. Michael's mommy cried quiet tears. Not loud wet wails like those he made that hot afternoon when his knees skidded on the driveway. She painted his raw skin with a brush dipped in Merthiolate and covered it with a cloth bandage strip. Her long fingers tickled the soft skin under his arms. She puckered her lips funny and made a purring sound. He giggled with tears soaking his face, the sad and happy mixed together. After that, he ran off to play.

Michael said it in his head before he said it out loud. "Mommy, what's wrong?"

She crouched beside him and messed his hair. "I'm proud." She put her hands on his shoulders, then dabbed her eyes with the sleeve of her white blouse.

Michael saw no connection between his mommy's pride and tears, but this wasn't the first time he was unable to decipher her. He hoped she'd feel better by the time he and Linda walked home for lunch.

Other mommies and their six-year olds hovered by the entrance door with the sign that said Grade One. Michael surveyed the concrete play surface they stood on. A hopscotch grid painted in bright yellow lines lay unused. Children in jackets with matching clothes clutched their mommy's skirts like something dreadful was about to happen. This wasn't what he expected. Over the summer, his sister played pretend school with him. He already knew he'd have the same teacher Linda once had, Mrs. Dupuis.

She appeared on the doorstep beside two other teachers. Michael's eyes lit. She looked exactly the way she did in Linda's class picture. She held up a paper and adjusted the eyeglasses attached to a chain around her neck. Calling the children's names, she asked them one at a time to gather in a row. She waved her hands, drawing stray children back in line, a traffic director of little people in new shoes.

The students were arranged in rows once again, this time with their hands clasped on top of their desks. Mrs. Dupuis announced they'd get to know each other on the first day. That meant the children should stand one by one and say their names. Since Michael's desk was third down in the first row, his jitters came and passed by fast.

He focused on the others. Some called out their names as though they personally chose them, others opened their mouths like withered snapdragons. Michael wasn't sure which category he belonged to, if either. He wished he had what it took to achieve something and be good too.

The bell announcing lunch sounded more like an angry cartoon buzzard than a musical instrument. Michael stood outside his classroom door waiting for Linda. On the way home, she held his hand as they crossed the street separating the school from Creekwater Bay, and didn't let go until they reached their house. It wasn't the rule to hold his sister's hand. He was too old for this, but loved her warmth finding its way into his. She was almost as beautiful as his mommy.

two

Saturday night. Awake past bedtime. Bursts of chatter and laughter slid under his bedroom door, and Michael strained to hear the Perry Como album playing on the Hi Fi. He and Mommy loved the words to that song. They were the next best thing to a picture book, though he'd never been to a penny arcade or a Halloween hop.

"Magic Moments." He liked how the *ma* went down low and rose again for *gic*. Mommy played the song Sundays after church when Daddy went to meet friends at the golf course or get caught up on work at the office. Mommy said not to tell she lifted the needle's arm to put it back to the same place over and over. He held her wink sacred.

After hearing the forty-five she brought home with the pretty dress and shoes yesterday, Michael might have considered it another favourite. The three ladies singing came through the speakers clear and sweet. But when Mommy danced, she seemed unhappy. She didn't ask him to sing along and the song's loudest words asked an angry question.

Michael sat up in bed. After the music stopped, the grown-up voices dimmed. Goodnights drifted through the wall. The front door thumped shut one last time.

His head fell forward, his eyelids slid down, and then snapped open like window blinds. The sound of his parents fighting shot into his room from somewhere out there, a scary telephone conversation. Daddy shouted *paranoid,* a word Michael didn't know, and then *ridiculous,* a word that meant stupid. His ears split as glass tumbled and smashed against the steel of the kitchen sink.

Mommy's sobs and Daddy's stomping feet slashed into his heart. He wondered whether he should come out of his room to help them, but Linda creaked open his door before he could. She slipped under the covers and lay beside him. The enemies under the bed would keep their mouths shut for now. He dozed in and out of reality. Linda watched the ceiling for bad things and patted his hands.

∼

An hourglass figure. Demure eyes. Class. James began his search for the perfect wife long before his parents knew he was dating. He loved many beautiful women before Francine. In '53, he vowed to deserve her until death parted them. Designed and built a home for her that stood above others.

Each year of their marriage James invested in a newer car, until he worked his way up to the '62 *Valiant*, white with a maroon band wrapped around it. He bought it imagining taking his family for Sunday drives on summer weekends, north to Grand Beach, or east to the Whiteshell. The only thing missing was a dog, its name Champ or Bud, head poking out the backseat window, long pink tongue flapping in the wind.

Francine turned out not to be much of a dog person. The only pet she agreed to keep was a budgie. Sometimes, when he came home from work, he'd set it free; watch its haphazard flight into furniture and potted plants, its struggle to land on the picture window curtain rod. The children's squeals eased his burdens, but he really did it for Francine's scolding. Her reaction made him a man.

Though he loved her, he found keeping his domestic promise hard. She was kind, real, honest, and too much the right woman for him. Sometimes he needed a taste of the wrong one. The first time James cheated on Francine he regarded his act as more indiscretion than infidelity. They were taking a break from going steady. Sleeping with his friend's sister felt wrong halfway through their sex. He closed his eyes and pretended Francine lay there under him, though she never had in those days.

The next time James slept with someone else, their wedding was only days away. The stress of living up to her parents' expectations left him vulnerable. The smoky-eyed broad came on to him in the bar after the guy he shared drinks with Tuesdays called it a night. She admired his hands, ran her fingers through his hair like a mother through her son's. Well before dawn, he woke in the flimsy bed to the smell of cigarette smoke. She sat naked; her backcombed hair disheveled against propped up pillows. He looked her in the eye, and then scribbled a fake phone number on a book of the motel's matches before walking out the door to the parking lot.

The time after that he betrayed a Francine pregnant with their third child. He broke down and told her the sordid details as they watched *The Tonight Show* in bed late one night. Confessing his shame didn't bring the relief he wanted.

The night Francine threw a party for him in honour of his award, he could honestly say he hadn't felt an urge to stray. She looked stunning, played her part to perfection. Knew exactly what was expected of her.

After the last guest left, he offered to clear the dishes. Her tone bit him hard. He responded quietly. She refused to let go, brandished her suspicions like a mugger with a switchblade. She threw a tray of empty cocktail glasses in the sink.

Anger grabbed him by the throat. "Goddammit woman," he said, and yanked her face close to his. "You think the money to buy those came easy?"

Francine shook his hold, snatched a goblet, and smashed it against the glass lying in the sink. The cracking sound fueled her rage. "Go to hell Jimmy." She marched to the kitchen door.

He took long steps toward her, spun her around. She struggled, and shook her head back and forth, a toddler too angry for words.

He took a deep breath, looked down to her barely showing belly, released his hands from her arms, and hung his head. "I'm sorry Francie, I'm so sorry. Forgive me."

Francine's blue eyes locked with his brown. She spoke through her teeth. "Whatever's between you and Dorothy has to end." She stomped toward the living room.

Ashtrays overflowing with butts littered the kitchen counter. A stream of smoke smoldered from one. James stood still, Francine's sobs drilling his ears. Her anger scared him. Her crying killed him. He thought he heard a door to one of the children's rooms open.

~

Their sandbox days began when they were three. Darren shared his pails and shovels with Linda. Together they built castles and moats, dungeons to throw prisoners in. She ran in flip-flops to her backyard garden hose, filled pails two at a time, and scurried them back to the playground. He told her she was his princess. And would rescue her if ever a dragon came to her doorstep selling Avon.

When he was five, Darren slipped her a valentine card. Linda gave him one too. His showed a boy whose shoe pulled at strings of bubble gum stuck to pavement. Her's read *Sweet-Hearted*. She'd torn out the children's page from *Better Homes and Gardens,* glued it to the back of a Cheerios box, and carefully cut along the dotted outline.

Linda was seven the morning Darren asked her to marry him. His grey eyes and white blond hair made her consider, but his bragging got in the way. Maybe he'd stop if she asked him to. Darren was sometimes very kind to her.

That same day he showed her the marks on the back of his shoulders and legs. Claimed he earned them daredevil cycling. But Linda's mommy said he must get beat by a belt. Darren told her about the club his dad belonged to. That she had to keep it secret. Mr. Amsel hated some kind of people. Darren was weak on the details.

The first time Darren cried in front of Linda, she gave away her eight-year-old heart. She sat holding his hand, and smoothed the hair from his eyes. Offered to say a prayer. His tears stopped like a faucet turned off tight. He clasped his hands together and mocked, "Save all the bad children in thy tender care."

That cloudy day at recess, Linda wished he'd disappear. The double-dutch competition needed her concentration. She finally mastered simultaneously moving her feet, escaping the two ropes before they hit the ground, and singing the skipping song.

In the middle of, "Soldier Sailor Beggar Man Thief," Darren appeared throwing pebbles at her penny-loafers. Linda was the first to know. She squeezed her lips together. Vivian caught on and ran to get the recess monitor, Mrs. Dupuis.

"Vivian says Darren has been throwing rocks at you Linda. Is that true?" Mrs. Dupuis moved one teacher shoe in front of the other.

Linda looked at Darren, who had already been strapped once the first week of school. She lied to save his hands from more pain.

The story about firecrackers going off in the boy's washroom showed itself in her mind like a television commercial. She could see him snickering, a row of the skinny red tubes in one hand and a pack of matches in the other. "I didn't feel anything."

"Why then would Vivian haul me all the way here?"

"I don't know. She doesn't lie." Linda sent a message to Vivian with her eyes.

Vivian spoke in her high-pitched voice. "I have to tell when kids hurt others."

Hands reaching out to the grade one girls by her side, Mrs. Dupuis shook her head. "Next time you see Darren hanging around, tell him to go play with the boys." The buzzer sounded, and she turned to walk away. Long rows of children formed at the school's side doors. The courtyard cleared as one teacher per line escorted them inside.

three

Michael sat beside Tommy Donovan in the sandbox. They were both seven and big fans of Popeye.

Across from them, Darren stood on the dandelion peppered grass. He shoved his hands into his pockets. "You sissies wanna get married."

Michael hung his head. His eyes surveyed the pebbles topping the sand.

Darren spat hard. "And I'll show you how to make a baby."

Tommy darted up. "You watch. I'll sic my brother Bruce on you."

Darren took a few steps back. "Bruce is a homo too. I would know." He pointed a finger at Michael. "Hey Buddy. Remember our deal." Darren turned and ran as though he'd fly into the hot sun.

Darren laughed like The Joker, Batman's enemy in the comics. Michael knew that man was bad to Batman and all good people in Gotham City. So why would Jesus expect Michael to be Darren's friend?

Michael wished he could be inside. It wasn't Mommy, but Auntie Stella who sent him out to play. She lived next door and was Penny's mommy. These days she watched Michael and Linda until their daddy got home for supper. She made sure his mommy lay in bed and ate Lipton chicken noodle soup with crackers or toast spread thick with honey.

Mommy returned from the hospital seven days ago without her big tummy and the baby she promised. Then stayed in her room to cry. Linda told Michael the baby's name was Randall and lived a little while. They were to call him Randy. There was only one picture of him. Mommy said he looked a lot like Michael when he was born.

Michael was stuck in the playground until supper, which was earlier these days because of Mommy. He wished he could take Tommy to his room so they could dig into his new set of Legos; he recently figured out how to lay a floor plan for his dream house. But Auntie would say no.

Linda and Jill skipped from the end of the path up to the sandbox. They sat on the wooden triangles set in its corners, hugging their knees to their chests. The breeze blew their hair from their faces the way paper fans do.

Compared to Linda, Jill wasn't pretty. Her curls stuck out like Slinky toys. Red blotches stained her skin. But Jill had a way of making Michael feel special.

Tommy stood and shouted to the sky. "If Darren comes around here one more time, I'm gonna get Bruce to whoop his butt."

Linda spoke with the voice of a teacher. "Whatever Darren does, getting worked up about it only makes him worse.

Tommy kicked up the sand at his feet. "Bruce could kill him."

Michael wished he could tell Linda about Darren's threats to his boy parts. The hard slaps to the side of his head, the punches in the stomach to make him stop crying.

But if he told, Darren said everyone would know he did dirty things and stop loving him.

What Darren insisted Michael do next terrified him - steal his daddy's cigarette case, the one with the built-in lighter, set a fire under his own bed, and put it out before getting caught. Darren demanded he see the charred floor for proof and promised to call on Michael to check. That's when the case was to be handed over.

Michael had the week before the first day of grade two to get the job done. Time was running out. He vacillated between allowing Darren's violations and lighting the small fire. Daddy would miss his special cigarette case.

~

The hurt Darren did to his body ripped into his head. Two days before grade two began, the enemies under the bed forced Michael to choose. He'd steal the lighter while his daddy ate breakfast in his terry towel robe. When Mommy had her afternoon nap, he'd sneak pages from the Sunday paper into his room. Long after Michael said his bedtime prayers and Linda closed his door behind her, the fire would be set. And put out before anyone knew. In the morning, after they ate porridge for breakfast, the two of them would walk to school. He hoped she'd hold his hand on the way. When Darren cornered him on the playground, Michael would give him the silvery case and invite him home to see the damage under his bed.

That night, the enemies were as scared as Michael. They could be badly burned. They crawled out from under the bed and huddled in the corners of the room. Michael already knew fire travels up, so he didn't need them telling him. He also knew how to start a fire, but this one was different. The frame of the bed hung low, making it impossible for him to fit more than his arms underneath. He lay on his side to look under. The dark made it hard to see his hands. And he had no kindling.

Michael decided to do it the way the enemies said to. He took three long Lincoln Logs, hooked them into a triangle, and then set five across its top. He nudged the structure along the hardwood floor and pushed it under the mattress with his fingertips. He crumpled the pages of the *Free Press* he'd kept hidden under his pillow, and shoved those against the logs.

The first few times Michael rolled his thumb along the lighter's ridged metal wheel, nothing more than a few sparks escaped. Next time, his thumb caused a hot blue flash. He let go fast and it disappeared. Again he jerked his thumb across the roller, held tight, amazed by the perfect baby flame, but let it die.

Sliding on his knees, he bent toward the bed's underbelly. Michael held the lighter at an angle, inched it toward the newspaper, and snapped his thumb. A flame shot up. He stared at its beauty. A quick release of his thumb and it was gone. A skinny wisp of smoke curled its way along the sideboard, and then dissipated.

He flicked the roller once more and watched the translucent orange travel over the surface of the paper. A smell of burning twigs mixed with chemicals pasted itself inside his nose. He drew in one deep breath and then another. Black smoke rolled toward him and burst into flame. He glued himself against the wall opposite.

More swirling clouds escaped from under the bed. The enemies choked and coughed. They waved at Michael to follow them out of the room. Hands covering their faces, they led him to the hall and into the living room. They banged their bodies against the front door and flung it open. Michael followed them down the driveway and toward the path leading to the playground. The enemies lined up at the swing set, each claiming a flat wood seat. Michael sat motionless on his, feet dragging. The enemies cackled. Pointing their feet up wildly, they yanked on the swing's chains to take them higher.

⁓

James coughed and gasped for air. His lungs heaved and hacked in waves. Francine clutched his shoulders and shook them hard. He dragged himself up and leaned against the headboard. A dark cloud hovered at the bedroom ceiling.

He pulled Francine into the hall. She stumbled behind as they made their way to Linda's room. He whipped open the door. Francine pushed past him and entered the white veil of smoke. She gathered Linda in her arms, threw her into his, and crashed her way to Michael's room. James stood transfixed. As she entered Michael's room, a wall of flame flashed and separated them. He hesitated for one surreal moment, and then ran, escaping out the already open front door with Linda in his arms.

James held his finger over the neighbour's doorbell, pounded and kicked their door. When Evan showed his face, James barked, "Call emergency." He shoved Linda forward.

James turned toward his house. Smoke pushed out from the front door. He scrambled his way to the back and smashed his body against it. The door loosed from its frame and fell with his furious stomp. The distant sound of sirens spliced through the fire's growl.

He toppled over Francine's crumpled body a few feet from the back entrance. Bent low, he dragged her along the floor. As he pulled her into the yard, James sensed an apparition standing over them. A masked fireman scooped up Francine and called for James to follow.

An ambulance wailed its way around the red pumper truck in front of the house and skidded to a stop. James watched two paramedics load the mother of his children into the ambulance. Slow-motion time.

The crowd of people gathered on the bay weren't real. James pictured Michael lying on his bed screaming in pain. Burning to death. He fell to his knees and banged his head into the concrete.

Evan pulled him to a stand. "I'll get you to the hospital. Stella will watch Linda."

James stared at Evan. An image of Michael's charred remains reflected back.

~

Michael wished he could be alone, but the enemies crowded so close he could hardly breathe. He could do nothing to change the truth. Sitting on the playground swing, he watched the house his Daddy built turn ugly.

The enemies cackled at the siren wails announcing the fleet's arrival. The creatures scurried back and forth down the path, peeking around the corner from behind a fence to give Michael updates. They described every detail of the shiny vehicles: ladders and hoses, hoses and ladders. To drown out their crowing, Michael pressed his hands over his ears. But he knew he was wrong to do it and dropped his hands like deadweights. The wind carried bits of information from the scene, muffled sounds of heroism and panic jumbled together.

The smell of choking found him. Mommy, Daddy, and Linda could never escape from that house. He watched the terrible burn act like the smaller fires Darren set. Clouds of rolling smoke announced the explosion of colour, flames stretching into ever-changing shapes.

Michael's tears refused to stop, even if they didn't deserve to fall. His lungs squeezed tight waiting for the police to find him and throw him in jail. The enemies said the officers were ready with handcuffs, but scattered when they saw Darren walking their way. He stopped in front of Michael and jiggled his hands in the back pockets of his pyjamas.

"You don't have to cry little man," Darren whispered. He tapped Michael's shoulder.

Michael stood up. Time to turn himself in. He handed the cigarette case to Darren.

Darren slid it into his pocket. "I've wanted this for years. Your dad too, but that's another story." Darren extended his hand. Michael accepted. "I'm gonna take you to your sister."

Linda. Not dead.

"Your dad went to the hospital. They took your mom away in an ambulance."

Mommy and Daddy. Alive.

"Get this straight," Darren said, clamping Michael's fingers, "Nobody knows I had anything to do with this. Or you die." He bent down and shoved his face into Michael's. "Linda too."

Before he heard it said out loud, Michael had not considered revealing Darren's role. Michael offered his hand

and let himself be led toward the bay. Darren seemed very brave. Compared to the coward he was.

Darren quickened his pace as they came into sight of the groups of neighbours huddled together. He smoothed Michael's hair, put his arm around his shoulder, and pulled him toward a man who looked to be the fire chief.

"This is Michael Ballantine, the boy who lives in that house. I found him in the park."

The chief nodded, and ran shouting to one of the firemen.

Stella appeared from behind and wrapped her arms around Darren. His body stiffened.

"Darren. You're a hero. You've done a good thing."

Michael felt unworthy of his sister's arms.

four

Miss Clancy marked an x over half the days on the grade two September calendar and Michael had still not been to visit Mommy in the hospital. He worried she wouldn't know where to find him now they were in a motel.

The enemies rode the horses in the painting hanging over the double bed his dad slept in, but refused to sleep under the bed Michael shared with Linda. They lurked in the dark hallways, followed him to school, into class, and slipped into his desk. The way they buzzed like houseflies under his stack of scribblers stopped him from concentrating on the teacher.

When Miss Clancy talked about numbers, the enemies belted out the theme song to *Petticoat Junction*. When she wrote on the chalkboard they leaped in front of his face. When she asked him to colour inside the mimeograph lines, they grabbed his pencil crayon and jerked it back and forth.

Miss Clancy began the year making soft eyes at him, but lost her patience as the weeks passed. She'd say "You did that on purpose," and "I need to talk to your father."

More and more, she carried out her threats. She couldn't know the enemies made themselves invisible and spoke in whispers too low for her ears.

Linda visited Mommy with Daddy once. When she returned, she sat Michael down. "She's in a burn ward. The doctors don't want children there much, because of germs."

"Does she want to see me?"

"She loves you. She says thanks for the picture and she liked the way you drew the trees."

"She has lots of bandages?"

"Mommy is wrapped in white. And wears a mask too."

"Can she see?"

"Yes. There are slits so she can see and talk. A little."

Michael wished he could ask Linda to deliver the letter Darren helped write and kept for him. The letter said he was a bad boy who no one should love. He was to blame, no one else, so he couldn't risk his sister opening the envelope. Once unsealed, the enemies might add something nasty.

Linda kept her voice quiet. "Mommy's eyes say she's sad."

Michael didn't need to ask. She was a lady who lost her pretty lashes. Darren said so.

At least Darren wouldn't drop by the motel they were staying in while they waited for their new place to be ready. Michael visited its construction sight once. His daddy talked to the builders about his house of dreams. The words came out so fast he sounded like a different man. And the wind carried his laugh to a far off place.

~

Francine spent weeks locked inside the hospital bed rails. She'd had no awareness of the sun's position in the sky. Sleep kept her in its waters most of the time. When she floated to the surface of consciousness, she shut her eyes and tried to will herself under, change the story in her nightmares, end the search for a boy lost on deserted, tree-lined streets. He called, "I'm not here. No, not here. No no no no. Here."

Michael had been born sensitive. She wanted to hold him again, tell him he did the right thing running out of the house. James insisted she take time to heal before he'd bring him to her.

Pain acted as a player in her dreams. Sometimes it came dressed in silk, more often it ran naked, howling. When Francine confided in an evening shift nurse, she attributed the specters to the narcotic delirium of painkillers.

Francine remembered little about the first days she spent in the white bed or what happened to bring her there. The fire's force, the thick arms dragging her out of the house, the blinding lights inside the ambulance. Voices crammed together outside its doors, but only James' cut through. "Hold on Baby." Later she wondered whether she imagined it.

Early the next morning she woke paralyzed by tightly wound binding, a corpse who lived. Tubes ran up and out to places she couldn't see. A white cap with a black stripe running across its edge crossed in and out of sight.

Finally the thin nurse became real and spoke. "You're awake." Alice was her name. She hadn't seen her after that. When asked, nobody seemed to know her.

Not James either, who had at first spent hours by Francine's side. She'd been barely aware of his presence. Later, in sporadic lucid moments, she caught glimpses of flowers in vases and cards on the bedside table. James said nothing about them. She didn't ask. His words when he got there, when he left, were promises to make things right. Start over. Move into the new development across the highway, close enough to the children's school.

Her hearing had been unaffected by the burns. But she strained to understand his words. Soon after she took them in, their meaning escaped her.

He leaned over the bed, positioned his face close to hers. "I'm here."

He came into a soft focus. "How did the treatment go?"

She turned her head from side to side.

"Incredible. Anything else?"

She held up her left hand, wiggled the gloved fingers.

"Dr. Tupine says you're lucky."

A part of Francine wanted to kiss him on the mouth, another screamed inside.

"Linda says she loves you. Michael too."

Francine read the lie in his eyes. He was holding something back.

~

Francine had been in no condition to know her innocent little boy tried to burn them all alive. The investigation said the house fire began in Michael's room, was set intentionally. James kept the truth to himself for months. When he finally told Francine what he knew, she looked at him blankly and walked toward the hospital room's window. When she refused to speak, he left.

And James couldn't figure the disturbing note sent in the mail. The red crayon script looked like Michael's work from before the fire, but under his innocent words a puzzling P.S. said something about parts of his body under attack. Weird.

Linda had been a sweetie and good thing, because Michael took a lot of energy. Time he wished he had but didn't. His son's fears, the teacher's phone calls were over the top. When James was his age, a leather strap hung beside the blackboard, a reminder your old man would give it to you twice as hard when you got home.

The three of them lived in the motel just down the highway from the old neighbourhood, so the kids could stay in their school. But it'd been no picnic: getting them there and back, packing lunches, securing babysitters, the piles of laundry. Keeping his employees in line. James squeezed in every spare chance to have the new home built before Francine's discharge.

The Creekwater house would be restored and on the market soon. He anticipated having it off his hands in a month or less. The basic design remained. The minor changes focused on those selling features with the biggest payoff.

He took the children to inspect the work. Big mistake. Linda kept quiet while he spoke to the painters, but Michael insisted on whimpering and clinging to her skirt. He shivered as though some devil lurked around every corner. And only after she practically pushed him inside.

"I can't."

"There's nothing to be afraid of."

"I'll wait outside."

"Come see what Daddy's done."

Michael stretched his neck to one side and held his head in place, as though he could shut himself out of the picture. Linda stroked his back. Tears dripped down his face.

James took the lead. Linda took her brother by the hand. They walked through the kitchen and into the living room. Aside from a drop cloth rolled up in a corner, the room was bare. The floors were covered with a carpet that left footprint trails. One shade lighter, its white bounced off the walls. The hallway and bedrooms gave off a similar light.

When Linda pulled Michael to the door of his old room, he yanked his hand from hers and walked away. She looked to James and they followed him outside to the back yard. Michael stood like a pole in the ground. He repeatedly opened and closed his eyes, a tiny tin man. He whispered low; at first Linda didn't catch what he was saying. "d.f.b. d.f.b. d.f.b. d.f.b. d.f.b." A breeze picked up a scatter of yellow leaves and dropped them by their feet.

Michael begged James to take him back to the motel. Said he wanted Sugar Pops, the seventh day in a row. Though cereal wasn't on the dinner menu, the silver-haired waitress always made an exception for him.

Whenever Michael gave his order, she'd act like they just met. She'd slide her glasses down her nose and peer over them. "My favourite too." His eyes sparkled like all was right with his world for a flash of time. "You have an angel's face. What did you say your name was?"

They stopped at the construction site of the new house before heading back to the motel. In the lot next to the two story wood skeleton, a fresh excavation called out. Linda took hold of Michael's shoulders when he teetered close to its edge.

"Let's take a look." She pointed to the man-made pond at the border of the field behind the property. James nodded yes when she turned to him for permission. Linda skipped down the gradual slope toward the water and called for her brother to follow. He took off like a rabbit. James exhaled and smiled. The Michael he knew before the fire.

~

James would bring the children by later in the day. Francine slid her arms from under the bed sheet and lay them straight. Lines of reddened tissue wound their way up to her shoulders like ropes. She hadn't seen the scars on her face, but imagined they looked the way they felt under her fingertips. Leathery patches crudely stitched in place.

Leslie came dressed in a turquoise smock. She stood beside Francine, and placed the mirror in her hands, the kind used in beauty salons, oval and heavy. Magnifying.

The eyes in the glass looking back at Francine sparked cobalt blue streaks.

Leslie wrapped her hand around hers and supported it under the mirror's weight. "It's a lot to take in."

Francine's reflection shivered in disgust. "My face is hideous." She laid the mirror upside down on her lap.

"Some of the redness will fade. The contours will stay." Leslie's words were penitent. As though she were responsible.

Francine shook her head and handed the mirror back. Leslie left the room.

She got out of the bed and shuffled in slippered feet toward the window. A long row of parking meters lined the street below. Elderly oaks graced the adjacent park, and behind that sat the border of an old residential neighbourhood.

A wave of cold shot up her spine. She stood transfixed. Ordinary people walked by and took the summer sky for granted. A long time later she watched James pull up and park the car on a side street. He held the children's hands. She raced her fingers through her tufts of hair and hurried to pull a cap over her skull.

They appeared at the doorway of the private room. James drew in his lips. Michael stood holding Linda's hand. She nudged him forward. He dashed to Francine and buried himself in her white gown.

She put her arms around his sobbing body. "Sweetie. I missed you so much." She pried his face from her legs. "Let me look at you."

Michael hid his face in his hands. He seemed more like his father now. Arms and legs sprouted from his torso as though they replaced a first set. She fell in love with the new version of her son, but something was missing.

five

Michael began a new grade in school. Slept in a new bedroom in a new house in a new neighbourhood. So far, the enemies hadn't found him there. Maybe the streets surrounding Starling Drive, every one of them named after a Manitoba bird, confused them.

Mommy shared a bedroom with Daddy again. They whispered secrets to each other. His daddy kissed his mommy on the mouth for a long time. And said, "I love you," before he took his lips away. That made her cry. Maybe kissing hurt her lips. The fire turned them into shoelaces.

For a while she let Michael eat Sugar Pops and cream for breakfast on school days, and then started serving real food. Porridge. Shredded wheat. Boiled eggs and toast. He rode the bus to school and back. Linda kept him safe. Most days she squished up against him. If she sat beside friends instead, she found a place for him close to the driver.

He made a new friend who lived two houses down, Lee. They tested their skills on the playground structures. Michael liked the monkey bars. He propelled himself from bar to bar, his feet never touching the ground. But hated the teeter-totter. The more force the rider on the ground exerted, the harder the rider in the air slammed down.

Michael invited his mommy to ride the swings. He remembered the days in the old playground. She'd pump her legs until the swing chains seemed to detach themselves. He imagined she had wings, a dragonfly queen landing in a patch of clover.

Michael pleaded with her to come outside. "Mommy please. I want a swing race." He intended to let her win. Knew what she was missing: the teeny frogs that sprung up at every step, the foxtail bouquets, and the spray of the lake's fountain when the wind picked up.

"Sweetie. Why don't you ask Linda?"

"Because I want you."

"I'll watch you from the kitchen window." She held out her hand like she couldn't find the words to say no. He led her out the back door and to the park's tallest swing set.

On the count of three, Michael and Francine pushed off with their feet in the sand. He pulled the chains back, setting his head low to the ground, and stretched his legs. He looked to see Mommy do the same.

She laughed. "I'll catch up to you Batman. And when I do, you'll be sorry."

By exaggerating his pull back, Michael only pretended to find his way up.

Mommy glanced at him between her own upswings, caught up to him in two passes, and then flew beyond with two more. Her toes pointed like a ballerina's. She called to the fluffy white clouds. "I just might jump right about now."

White teeth flashed between Mommy's leathery lips. A picture of her laughing in a heap in the grass below showed itself in Michael's mind, but the dog at their feet erased it. The curly-haired creature came out of nowhere, growling and snapping. Mommy said to keep swinging. The more the dog barked and hopped on its short legs, the more she laughed.

The dog's owner scrambled from far across the park and whisked him up. He scolded the dog, and then stepped back. Michael and his mommy made their descent. And sat with dangling arms.

The man opened his eyes wide under the tam perched on his head. First, he stuttered something Michael couldn't hear. "Terribly sorry about the dog. I named him Kade, after my father. Just my luck, they're like each other." The man cleared his throat.

Mommy spoke in her sad voice. "What breed?"

"Who, the dog or the man? Actually, they're both Scottish. Well, I won't bother you. Sorry about my ill-mannered friend."

Michael wondered why the man seemed sorry and frightened at the same time, and whether Mommy noticed. On the way back to the house, her nose dripped.

"Let's not mention this to Daddy. Okay?"

~

Michael's new bedroom offered more space for his bins of toys. A little while ago, Auntie Stella from the old neighbourhood gave him three building sets as house-warming gifts. He wondered why, since he wasn't worthy. But that didn't stop him from working on his ideas. A week after he opened the packages, he'd created the start of a miniature suburb. Though he wasn't sure what, it seemed to him something was missing besides people and their cars.

He stepped over and around his work on the bedroom floor. When away from the site, he covered it with towels and keep out signs. Michael spent two top secret Saturday mornings adding a library and a barber shop.

He wiggled his way through lunch when they got home from church Sunday, and then invited his parents and sister to his room. With a big bite of fried egg sandwich crowding his mouth, he told his mommy he'd removed the spread from his bed. But couldn't tell her why. Sometimes the look on Mommy's face said she was looking at a ghost. But this time she shared a sunny smile with Daddy.

Mommy, Linda, and Daddy followed him up the stairs. Michael entered the room, leaving them jammed into the doorframe. He admired the bumpy terrain under the cover, and turned to face his audience. Linda stepped in to grab two corners of the spread while he held on to its opposite edges.

"One, two, three lift off." They parachuted the blanket up.

He watched his daddy's face, but caught only a glimpse of what he wanted to see.

"Hey Buddy, you're a chip off the block." Daddy kissed Mommy on the cheek. "You were right Honey." Daddy stayed awhile, pointed out the things he liked best, and then took Mommy into the hall. "Got some work to catch up on." He said it again, louder, like he had to convince her he wasn't lying.

Linda's eyes said sorry to Michael. She lowered herself cross-legged to the floor and sat on the perimeter of his project. "Which house would you live in?"

Michael pointed to a three story steel-girded structure rising above the others.

"Why that one?"

He was surprised she didn't know. Steel can't burn.

"What do you call this place?" she asked.

His heart beat fast and he lied. "Happy Family Place."

"I like it," Linda said. "But you have another name for it."

⁓

Linda took a long time to make her choice, and then bought the one with the single red rose on its cover. The dewdrops on its thorns drew her to it; that, and the fact it came with a tiny lock and key. She sat on her bed and pulled the small notebook from the plastic Kmart bag.

She opened the book to the first page and spread it flat, her pointer finger pressing against the binding. Here was a friend she could confide in. A place she could reveal the truth about her family. She jumped up to get a pen from the desk drawer and plunked herself back on the bed. The words flowed neatly from the pen.

Dear Diary,

My little brother is special. Michael has always been different. He has gifts he never asked for and maybe doesn't want.

My brother's eyes invite you in and shut you out at the same time. They look out of focus, dreamy, but scared of imaginary things he tells only me about. And describes them in ways so real, I can almost see them too.

If I had to sum up Michael in one word, it would be hurt. I want to take it away, but can't because that's what he's made of. It's as though a magnetic field he's defenseless to fight against surrounds him. I'm the only one who understands this. Not our mom, not our dad.

Michael draws designs in his head and puts them on paper like they came from someone else. From somewhere else. The past. The future. This impresses our dad. He tells Michael he'll grow up to be a genius architect. Our mom says God made Michael sensitive.

She's right. I'm here to protect him. I know Michael. Better than he knows himself.

Linda closed the book. She'd need a place to keep it where no one would think to look. Her next entry would be about a different subject. Darren.

Michael knew about the diary from its first page, but said nothing. Linda's hiding place was obvious, the tiny lock easily picked. A brother shouldn't read his sister's secrets, but this case was different. She was normal. He wasn't, and was looking for clues.

~

Linda turned fourteen two days before Darren kissed her for the first time. He talked her into skipping the bus ride home from school. They walked across the highway and stopped at 7-Eleven for Slurpees.

While they waited for the light to turn, his mouth surprised hers, wet and forceful. She never expected his face against hers, examined the contour of his closed lids, and considered pulling away. He seemed vulnerable, eager, and she didn't have the heart.

He stepped back, a strange mix of smugness and tenderness. He reached out to stroke her hand, swore her to secrecy. She left her hand in his until they reached the store.

They stood in front of the drink fountain.

"I'll buy you one." Darren picked up two large cups and handed one to her. "What kind do you want?"

"Oh you don't have to. Have one yourself."

"I want you to." He leaned in close. "You're getting Cherry Cola. That's what you taste like."

Linda blushed. She watched the clerk tap his fingers hard on the counter. Her neck twitched. She gave Darren a not-here look, but he couldn't read her unease. Or chose to ignore it.

He paid and they turned to leave. He half mumbled, half sang the words to a song about handing over some love. One arm pointed the way out; the other held open the door. "After you."

Without permission, a smile slid across her face.

They walked the short distance to the field behind her place, sat side by side on the swings, and finished their melting drinks. Linda twirled the straw in her cup. She felt Darren's eyes say things she shouldn't know. She knew her parents would be upset if they knew.

~

Francine set the pots to soak in the sink and looked out the kitchen window. Linda sat on the park swings, beside a boy she didn't recognize, tall and blonde. They pointed their feet toward each other and reached out with playful hands. The boy stood with his back to her and blocked the view of her daughter. His form drew a vaguely familiar picture. Must be an Amsel. He grew two feet since she saw him last. Darren was his name, poor child. Long strands of angel hair swished around the back of his neck. Francine felt like a spy and looked away.

The unlocked back door clicked open and she busied herself sorting cutlery, keeping her eyes on the tray. "Who were you talking to outside? Someone from school?"

"Yes." Linda looked at the cup in her hand. She blurted out a name like she picked it from the air. "Bruce Donovan. Tommy's brother? From Creekwater?" Her eyebrows furrowed. Almost imperceptibly.

Francine studied Linda's face and played along. "He seems nice. Why don't you invite him here sometime."

～

The first week of Junior High was behind him. Michael shoved his feet into his track shoes and slipped out the back door early Saturday morning. He headed to 7-Eleven before his parents could get out of bed. Even the field birds were groggy and made little effort to fly off at his approach.

The only other customer in the store was a taxi driver. He and the clerk talked to each other like they were long lost friends. Michael picked up a stash of penny candies from the row of plastic bins, filled a paper bag with Neapolitan taffy and jawbreakers. It brought back memories of the elementary school farewell party just before summer break.

The teacher showed a film. When the lights were on again, Miss Wicks let them listen to forty-fives. Side one of his contribution skipped too much and had to be turned over. The kids giggled listening to the flip side's love song. Michael wondered how it would feel slow dancing with a girl, but threw out the idea before anyone could read his thoughts.

Then the first day of grade seven happened and he was faced with Darren again. He ordered Michael to meet him after last class that same day. As he stepped around the corner leading to the school's backyard, he watched Darren press Linda against the outside wall of the music room. Their fingers interlocked, she held tight to his waist. Michael whisked around and ran the mile home. He left the back door open and raced upstairs to his room.

"Michael." His mother tapped on the door. "Have you seen Linda?" She was silent for a moment. "Why are you late coming home?"

Michael shook with rage on his bed. "No, haven't seen her. I'm not that late. Talked to the gym teacher about signing up for floor hockey."

"I'm worried about your sister."

"She'll take care of herself." He was sure his mother heard hate stain his words.

The doorbell rang and she left. The voices of Linda and his mother stirred together.

six

Moving between his grade seven classes, Michael straggled behind the others in the crowded hall.

Darren came from nowhere and pushed his chest into Michael's. "Ballantine, I can't believe it's you."

Michael looked behind himself, and then over Darren's shoulder to the end of the hall.

"Can't get over how much you still look like your sister."

The words in Michael's head swam in circles and refused to speak. A silly sound puffed out.

"Hey, I'm not gonna hurt you." Darren reached up and messed Michael's hair.

Michael stood like a broken fence.

Daren smirked. "Yeah, there's a bad moon!" His sentence dropped short.

"I gotta get to Math." Michael made a motion to move past.

Darren pushed into his chest again. "Later."

Michael's feet shuffled one in front of the other down the polished tiles. Darren's cold eyes trained on his back.

~

Francine spent the morning in Michael's room trying to organize his clutter. He kept his treasures in any kind of container he got his hands on: margarine tubs, milk cartons, shoe boxes. Sometimes he headed to the shopping centre to ask for used packing boxes.

An icy light illuminated the walls. Francine stood on tiptoes and drew her pointer along the dusty film covering the things on his closet shelf. She sighed and turned away. Kneeling on the floor, she bent down to stick her nose under the bed and scooped out a tissue box. As she swatted the dust ball on top, some paper scraps stuffed inside escaped and swirled to the floor.

She reached out to retrieve one. A strange, blue script covered it. Hardly a trace of white existed between the words. What seemed to be sentences, but may have been series of unrelated words strung together, overlapped, and swayed from side to side. Crammed together at the bottom of the page, each line broke free as it rose in a curve. Tiny question marks were scattered over them. What a strange diary her son kept. Song lyrics. Poetry. Whatever they were, their intent, their message was beyond her reach.

She sat on the bed and flattened several of the notes on the spread. Read and re-read each. Together, the words made no sense. Some flashed out repeatedly. Enemies. Whispers. Screams. One hid in the center, drawn in a faint hand. Fire.

Francine stood up and walked to the window. Outside, the pond sat frozen in patches beside the empty playground. A pair of stupid Canada Geese struggled for one last swim. Fatigue pushed over her, and she wanted to lie down. Pass out and escape. She slid one of the papers in her blouse pocket, left the room and closed the door.

Michael spent his first year in junior high a prisoner to the fear of what might happen. If grade seven was a tormentor, grade eight was the bully who grabbed him by the throat and carried out his threats. He was convinced Darren stayed behind an extra year by failing on purpose. The mind control began before the buzzer jolted Michael through the school doors in the morning and kept on after it spewed him out. Every day, Darren pressed his steel eyes against the glass windows of Michael's classes. And every day, they spoke.

Darren's eyes had dials that ramped up the volume, fast forwarded, and rewound. The voices looped circles in Michael's brain. The whispers were worst and scared off his efforts to have thoughts of his own.

They sounded like the enemies who hid under his bed when he was a boy, and asked him to draw up a death plan. Burn his family alive.

～

Most of the guys in the gym's makeshift cafeteria lived across the highway too. Michael sat on the same bench in the same spot every lunch hour. He pulled two peanut butter sandwiches, an orange, and some oatmeal cookies from a brown paper bag, and placed them on the table.

George always sat across from him. Michael was fascinated by his accent, his underground history, and an escape from Czechoslovakia.

George and his brothers entertained Michael in their basement on Saturdays. George and Pavel played guitars, Milos, drums.

"Something wrong about your eyes?" George leaned across the table, put his face close to Michael's, a secret-teller tactic.

Michael felt George's breath against his skin, and snapped to attention. The words filtered through.

"What do you mean? What about my eyes?"

"Your eyes, they are stuck, like those of a frightened cat."

Michael couldn't confide in George, not in front of these guys, not even if they were the only two there. Two tables over, Darren's eyes said to keep his conversation tight, then elongated and became those of a wolf. Darren held an apple to his mouth. The sound of his snapping teeth cut into Michael's ears.

"Nothing's wrong with my eyes"

"Then you are thinking about girls?"

"No." Michael picked up a cookie, turned it over, and put it down. "Shut up."

Tom elbowed Michael in the ribs. He laughed with a chunk of banana between his teeth. "The chicks think about you."

Michael's cheeks flushed.

Darren slid the remnants of his lunch to the girl beside him and got off the bench. Eyes on Michael, he stood clutching the girl's shoulders from behind. Bending over, he rubbed his head against hers. The girl turned to tap at his chest. Darren laughed with her and again to himself.

"What are you thinking Michael?" Looking for clues, George surveyed the room.

"I'm thinking the bell's gonna ring in the next thirty seconds."

Michael accompanied George to the locker room, the water fountain, and all the way to French class, every one of the five minutes they were late worth it.

~

Linda and her friends stood across the street from the 7-Eleven and waited for two cars to pass by. Darren burst out its doors, fireworks in jeans. She wished she could have him to herself again. But after weeks of meeting each other in secret places, he'd shut her out without saying why. Bruce stepped in to pick up the pieces and she let him. He held her hand like she was his accomplice.

Darren wore a skimpy leather jacket with a fur collar. He stepped up to a girl who stood by the phone booth on the wall beside the doors. She held a long skinny cigar between her thumb and pointer finger. The girl next to her tapped her platform shoes together, sending the snow sticking to their sides flying. She smoothed her hands over her frizzy curls.

Darren nodded his head as Linda and her friends approached the store. Bruce stayed outside in the parking lot. Darren walked up to him like he had bad news. Linda went inside with Janet and Sherry.

The three girls exited with Slurpees. Linda handed one to Bruce.

"Hey Linda, where've you been hiding?" Darren put on the voice he saved for her.

"I've been around." She looked back and forth between him and Bruce, and giggled.

Bruce laughed, shuffled his feet, and shoved a hand in his pocket.

Darren winked at Bruce. "You're lucky. I've been there too."

"Take care man." Bruce raised his cup to Darren then motioned for the girls to follow him.

Darren snatched the cup from his hand and took a long drag through the straw. "Yeah and you too Linda."

Bruce latched onto Linda's waist. She swatted his mittened hand with hers. Darren turned his back and they walked away.

"Creepy," Janet dragged out the word. "Why did you waste your time on him?"

"Darren's cool." Bruce drew Linda close. "He asked about you."

"Like I said." Janet swapped her Slurpee for Linda's.

The four of them spent the next hour aimlessly walking the deserted suburban bays.

Bruce dropped Linda off at her doorstep. "Darren says you know how to put out a fire?" He sounded apologetic.

"I have no idea why he'd say that except to be a jerk."

~

Darren's eyes showed themselves against the outside of Michael's bedroom window every night, curtains drawn or not. Sharp grey beams replaced their irises. They told him to do what they said and scoffed when he refused.

The eyes blinked rhythmically every few seconds, and then popped open wide like shorting neon signs. "Come on little fella, get it right. Don't screw up this time."

Michael whispered, "Why do you want to hurt my family? You're sick."

"Buddy, who's sick? You talk to eyes."

Michael answered their taunts for hours, and then rolled out of bed. Dragging his pillow and comforter behind him, he headed downstairs. Darren's eyes flew along behind. They jiggled up and down, snickering. Michael switched on the television and threw himself on the living room sofa. No picture appeared, just static, lit up snow. The eyes hovering over the console watched his sink behind their sockets.

~

By morning, Francine found him tangled in his comforter on the sofa. The dark circles under his eyes wouldn't let her wake him for school. She'd hold back her tears until James left for work. Linda would be up soon, make breakfast, and explain her brother's behavior. James bought it less and less.

They ate in an uncomfortable silence. "Take the boy to a doctor," James grabbed his coat from the front door closet. "I love you."

Francine kissed her husband on the cheek. "Love you too."

Francine let the morning and part of the afternoon go by before she sat beside her son and shook him awake. He rolled over and covered his head with the comforter.

"Gotta let me sleep. Tired."

"Michael, I made an appointment for you. You have another hour."

"Told you, not going."

"Your father wants this."

Michael curled in a ball.

~

Every day following the doctor visits seemed the same as the one before. Michael slept them away. James left for work, and Linda for school. Today was different. Francine pulled a black wool toque over Michael's head and wrapped its matching scarf around his neck. Halfway into January, the Christmas gift hadn't been worn.

His expression pained when she met his eyes. Francine's heart pushed to keep him home. She nudged him out the door and prayed the pills he took every morning for a month would keep him safe.

She closed the door behind Michael, secured the deadbolt, and turned to the hallway mirror. Her left eyelid drooped; the right peeled back, her skin, patches of brown on white. What looked like rows of string burrowed beneath the surface of her cheeks. Punishing herself wouldn't bring her any closer to understanding.

Now that Michael was in school, she could spend the morning in his room searching through his things. The drawings were new. Sketch after sketch of eyes that lived on paper. The same set, dispassionate, flat, staring through windows, detached from faces, no clues who they belonged to. They weren't his, the pupils, dark lead, the irises, three shades of grey, the eyelashes, separated and thin.

Francine gathered the sketches in a pile and stashed them behind the boxes of building sets on the closet floor. One sketch went into her housecoat pocket to tuck between the pages of her bible. And keep company to the note she stole from the tissue box hidden under his bed.

Darren exited the school lot, sped onto the road, and swerved to pass a car in his path. Linda sat wedged between him and his friend in the front seat. Curtis told Linda to call him Rooster. He bragged how he snatched his dad's car earlier that afternoon and let Darren drive the '66 *Chevelle* because he owed him. Since they found Linda walking home alone they might as well have offered her a ride.

She got in the baby-blue car without thinking, and now her nerves stung with a mix of fear and exhilaration.

Darren stole a look at her. "Got everything under control."

She pointed down the road at a parked car. "Watch it." He passed it, and she let some time go by before speaking again. "I'll walk home."

"Why did you get in the car if you didn't want the ride?" Darren put his arm around her shoulder.

She let it sit there, leaned into him. "You're scaring me. Slow down."

Rooster laughed. He rolled his window down and stuck out his hand like he was catching baseballs.

Darren rested his head against Linda's. "I wouldn't do anything to hurt you." He took his arm off her shoulder and slapped his knee. "I wanna take you somewhere."

"Let me out. Please. I have to get home." Linda sat up straight.

Darren reached around her shoulder and pulled her back. "I'm not going to let you go again. I'll take you home as soon as you see what I wanna show you."

Curtis rolled up the passenger window. "Geezus, it's cold."

Darren stopped at the highway intersection's red light. He pulled an illegal left and headed east. The car's speedometer reached eighty-five, ninety, ninety-five, racing several miles past the city limits. Darren hit the brakes and made a sharp right onto a service road. Clouds of snow engulfed the car as it shot down the gravel path.

"Where is it, where is it?" Darren stopped the car, looked over his shoulder, and backed up. "Here we are." He turned onto a narrow road lined by tangled pines.

"Cripes Darren." Curtis left his laugh back on the highway. "Easy on the car."

Darren pulled into a clearing towered by trees at the end of the road. In its center, a circle of rocks formed a fire pit. Blackened logs poked through the snow. Brown beer bottles littered its edges.

"Let's get out." Darren turned off the ignition, jammed the keys into his pants pocket, and whipped opened the door.

Curtis rolled out the passenger's side. Linda slid past the steering wheel and followed Darren. She closed the door carefully. Curtis mimed an exaggerated motion of slamming his door shut, and then imitated Linda's precision.

The three stood in the silent winter forest. With hands stuffed into their jacket pockets, they contemplated the abandoned pit.

"My paradise." Darren stepped sideways, close to Linda. "I'll bring you here alone one night. I'll start a fire. And get you buzzed." He held an imaginary joint to his lips.

"I have to go home. My mom worries."

"Promise you'll come back with me." He withdrew a hand from her pocket, held it tight, his eyes piercing hers.

"If you take me home."

"Fire first."

Dear Diary,

He set a fire in a cold and quiet place I didn't know about. We sat side-by-side on the trunk of a fallen tree and stared at it, laughing every time a spark popped our way. I could see his heart peeking out from behind his words, too shy to show itself in front of his friend.

I'm in love with the little boy who shared half a stick of his bubblegum before asking me to be his wife. He's the best secret I've ever kept.

seven

James pounded his fist on the kitchen table. The mug in front of him jumped, splattering coffee on the white tablecloth. Francine shuddered. She inched over to the kitchen window and turned her back to him.

His voice slapped her from behind. "Goddammit Fran. I don't want to hear it. Our children are messed up. Linda lets boys use her and Michael doesn't know fact from fiction. Show our girl what it means to be a woman. And let the boy grow a set of balls. Half his problem is your smothering. Three guesses what the other half is?"

Francine spoke to the floor. "Don't have any." Heat rose from her chest to her throat. She stretched her eyes to the ceiling. The words gusted out. "You must know. Considering how much time you put in with him. Tell me."

James shot up from his chair. "You, you, and bloody you, Fran."

Francine braced herself against the counter and shouted at the view beyond the glass. "Stop blaming me. Stop blaming me." Squeezing the counter's edge, she bent over the sink like she might vomit, and then flung herself up.

A detached Francine stepped aside and watched another self lose control. "Go to hell go to hell." The real Francine snatched a bowl from the sink and smashed it to the floor. The other shook her head and clucked her tongue.

James grabbed the chair, and banged it on the floor. "Take a look at yourself in the mirror."

Francine cried out.

"For Christ's sakes, quit using your face as an excuse. The fire was years ago. Get over yourself." James cleared his throat and lowered his voice. "I have to leave. Calm down will you."

Francine ran past him and upstairs to the bathroom. She slammed the door shut and locked herself in. Propped against the door, she listened to the sound of his car start and drive away.

She stood, faced the mirror, and crooked her fingers like claws at its reflection. She yanked her hair in jerking motions, punched the counter beneath her, and lifted her hand in pain. The softest part of her palm swelled fat and red. She sat on the toilet bowl cover, cried until her eyes stung, and then got up. There was housework to do, a shattered bowl that needed to be swept.

Francine dropped the shards from the dustpan into the kitchen garbage tin and looked around the room. For a long time she lost herself rearranging cupboards, but grew suddenly weary, and sat at the table. Across from her, the wet in her eyes blurring its image, the painting on the wall seemed to speak. A wild rose crammed the entire surface of the canvas. She'd painted it years ago, cerise, not the true colour of the flower.

Francine sat transfixed. She longed to return to her easel, record the images of her inner world. Shades of deep plum, musty blues, brown-infused purples, and greens tinged with yellow edges. The life cycle of bruises portrayed in the language of flowers.

Irises. She'd give birth to blackened flowers awakening on a forest floor. First she'd sketch them in a tangled clump beneath an elderly oak. Then paint the damp rotting ground of their sacred space.

Francine was sick of the struggle. Uncertainty puddled in place of anger. Acted as truce between James and her self-hatred. Whether she was weak didn't matter. Her art made life fair.

As a little girl, she lived a protected life. A mother who taught her the social graces, an older brother whose accomplishments threw comforting shadows. Her father provided a respectable home, private schools, music lessons, and a cottage at Lake of the Woods. On summer vacations they spent long hours alone paddling a canoe on evening waters. He said she was his rose petal. Some flowers need special gardens to grow.

She once believed she provided that garden for her own children. But Linda was a wild daisy flourishing in a highway ditch, Michael, an orchid cowering among weeds. When Francine first held Linda, she gazed at the hospital ceiling lights like they were stars. Michael squeezed his eyes shut, afraid to live outside the dark of her womb.

Dear Diary,

When they think I can't see, my mom and dad look at each other with invisible darts. Mom says things to him she thinks I won't catch - clues about chasing other women. She's right. I see the way he looks at them.

~

The heat of her flawless skin against his. His chest pounding into the cushion of her breasts. He owned her. Though she belonged to a man who lived a few streets over from his. He watched her pupils dilate when she called out, her body jerking like a feral cat. She made him say her name. Dorothy. Made him feel alive.

~

James had no access to Francine's affection. She wouldn't let him touch her, not in the way he wanted, not in the way she once did.

She judged herself by the looks thrown at her outside their home, not by the way he felt for her inside it. The scars fire imposed on her beauty couldn't keep him from being fascinated by it.

But she lived for the children. Especially Michael. The two were tied together by a pact. The boy who burned down his father's house and set his mother on fire. Not like his son understood the power he held. Michael crept through his days with the feet of a ghost. Francine fretted along behind. This was a day James would cry if he had the time.

More breakfast table drama. Another scheme to skip school.

Francine pushed a plate of toast toward Michael. "You hardly eat."

"I can't."

"You've missed so much school."

"I won't fail."

"You have another doctor's appointment soon."

James mumbled under his breath, "Damn useless doctor."

Neither Francine nor Michael acknowledged his anger. James pushed his chair back. He pictured himself giving the boy a hard shake, shoving him in a cold shower. Snapping him out of his coma.

Michael bolted upright from his chair. Screamed bloody murder enemies attack. Wide open panic eyes. Trembling hands and arms and body.

Francine wrapped her arms around him. "Tell me."

Like she bought it. Too goddamn much. James sat stunned, watched the scene play itself out. No words.

Michael spun toward the window like something waited for him out there, and when he saw what it was, collapsed. He squeaked like a dying mouse. Francine lowered herself to the floor. She gasped and sobbed.

James got out of his chair and pulled his wife to a stand. He wrapped strong arms around her, pulled his head back to see her face. "Don't cry like that." He patted her hair. "Not in front of the boy. Everything's going to be alright." He led Francine to her chair. "Believe me."

James attempted to drag Michael off the floor, but the boy held himself rigidly, dropped his chin to his chest, and pulled his knees tight against his body. James struggled to untangle his limbs.

"Think about what you're doing to your mother. Stand up dammit."

Michael opened his eyes. He went limp, and shook his head. "Sorry."

~

Their first time happened in the back seat of Rooster's dad's car. Darren wrangled it from Curtis in exchange for a nickel bag of pot. He'd set a fire in the pit. Close to the flames, they sat side by side on their fallen tree trunk. Snow heavy trees shut out the wind. But the bonfire's powerful heat couldn't keep the cold from claiming her bones.

He scooped her up on his lap like a baby, and she molded into his embrace. He lifted her face with fingers under her chin and pressed kisses on her forehead. Her hands clasped around his neck, she pressed her lips against his. He suggested the car - the engine running, the heater cranked, the window opened a crack. Linda let him lead her to the back seat.

She cringed at his hands exploring her bare belly and breasts. No one touched her that way before. She shivered and took stunted, shallow breaths. The word no stayed trapped inside.

His hands warmed. His half-smile said he thought he was pleasing her. He told her he loved her. She wasn't sure what he meant by that, but she loved him with an ache to erase his pain. She hoped he understood.

He pulled her jeans to her ankles and slid them off one leg at a time. Took off his own pants and threw them into the front seat. Linda chirped like an injured bird at the pain of his attempted entry.

Darren sat up, his legs straddling hers. "Am I hurting you? Want me to stop?"

Linda took a while before shaking her head.

"Wanna try again? I'll go slow."

Her head moved up and down.

Darren scattered small kisses on her face, what she really wanted. He lay on top of her, his weight compressing her lungs. He whispered that they belonged together. She played with his hair and asked him why he said that. Why did he love her and not someone else? He laughed.

Their second time happened under her parents' roof. While everyone else slept, Linda crept downstairs to the back door and slipped Darren into the rec room. She escorted him to the shag rug in front of the television and they sat cross-legged across from each other. He passed her the bottle in the brown paper bag he'd hid under his jacket, Cinzano, lifted from his parents' cabinet, and chosen because of the made in Italy label noosing its neck. They passed it back and forth, taking turns chugging what Darren called women's whiskey. The liquid burned sticky and thick down Linda's throat.

The television's light glowing on their faces, a soundless *The Midnight Special* played. Before the bottle had been halfway emptied, David Bowie began his strut on stage. Darren leaned over to cup his hands on the sides of Linda's face. They looked at each other for a long time, and then she leaned forward to kiss his nose. He surprised her with his lips laughing against hers.

They sprawled together on the carpet. Darren trapped her body between his legs, squeezing her arms hard. He bounced up and down, and as he did, something silver-tipped and rectangular poked out of his shirt pocket as though it might escape, but didn't. He swiped his hair back and forth across her face, rubbing his lips against hers with each pass. She turned her head from side to side. His bones cut into hers and she struggled to loosen his grip. He held her tight.

"Am I hurting you Linda?" He made mocking sounds as he slid off.

He crouched down beside her, and stroked her face. "I'm sorry. You make me this way. I'll take it easy."

Linda lay on the carpet, examined his eyes, and saw nothing there. She put her hand over the hand he held on her face. And kept searching.

Dear Diary,

I don't know what to think about Darren. I only know that I'm in love with the secret child hiding in me.

˜

Michael left the house letting his mom believe he was headed for school. At the time, he thought he was. But his walk stopped at the strip mall across the street at the end of the bay. He stood shivering by the Kmart entrance. During his wait for the store to open, the sky transformed from stone to cotton.

A blue-vested employee swung open the doors. The strong smell of cheap spray permeated her bleached hair. Her nametag read Dorothy and she smiled like she knew him. He walked past her, afraid she might be on to him. He methodically combed the store aisles and was unaware at what point they became those of a library. He searched for an ancient text on Gothic architecture, and then gave up, deciding the book had to have been checked out. The library shelves unfolded like a card trick and rearranged themselves into a steel-walled maze. Abandoning his shoes, he tiptoed in socks, counting each step he took.

Security stopped him as he made his way to exit a few hours later. His pockets held a bag of plastic forks, a box of wooden toothpicks, and a pack of pencils. Michael confessed the stolen merchandise were weapons that would skew the eyes of his enemies. He surrendered himself to the perfumed blonde. Dorothy paid the $1.81 he owed and walked out of the store with him.

~

The doorbell's call cut into Francine's thoughts. She peeked between the drawn curtains and saw Dorothy standing on the step, her arm laced through Michael's. Francine unlocked the deadbolt and pushed open the door.

Dorothy's face cringed in pity. Michael stared blankly. Like he no longer knew his own name. Dorothy told her story, but Francine barely registered it, held by the dark tint of the skin under her son's eyes, the ice clumps glued to his socks. She couldn't bear to hear more.

"Thank-you Dorothy." She pulled Michael inside and spoke through the door as she closed it. "He hasn't been himself. I'll take care of it."

He plodded along beside her up the stairs. Halfway to the top, he stopped and made his legs iron rods. Francine tugged him, but he yanked away and jerked himself around.

Francine reached for his arm. "Come to your room."

Michael bolted down the stairs. He ran the circular path connecting the kitchen and living room. Francine stood with arms outstretched, blocking his access to the kitchen, but he swung around in the other direction and ran. He swiped knick-knacks off the tables at either end of the sofa. Francine chased him like a dog after a cat, and then stopped, struggling to catch her breath. She lowered herself to her knees. Michael crawled up beside her and sat on his calves. He placed a hand on her back.

"Sorry Mom. I don't want to have to tell you. They'll get me."

Francine gulped for air. "Who'll get you? What's happening to you?"

"I don't want to get you involved."

Francine held his hand in hers. "Let me protect you." She led him to the sofa and sat him beside her. He laid his head on her lap.

Eyelids fluttering, he lay still. She smoothed his hair like she did when he was a little boy falling asleep in the car. Moments later he thrashed and howled in a single breath until his air depleted. As suddenly as the fit came on, it ended. Michael opened his eyes, and contemplated the ceiling as though he'd never seen one.

Francine looked for answers in his lost face. She led him upstairs to his room and into bed. He turned to his side and drew his legs up. With short, quick pulls, she removed his parka and his wet socks. She grabbed a blanket from the hallway closet and returned to cover him.

Sitting on the floor beside his bed, she clutched her knees. For a long time, there was no movement from Michael, no sound, as though he died when he lay down. She sat as still and soundless as he for what seemed an hour. Francine wondered whether it would be safe to get up and give James a call. On her own, she felt helpless.

She inched her way off the floor. Michael stirred under the blanket. She listened carefully to his muffled words.

"I won't do it. Don't. Set me on fire." He covered his face with both hands and let out little squawks of pain. She'd done the same back when she hadn't the strength to match the intensity of her cry to her agony. She lowered herself to the floor and kept her vigil.

Linda found her there when she returned from school. She called from the bottom of the stairs, and appeared at

Michael's bedroom door moments later. Linda looked at her sitting on the floor and at her brother in a tangled heap on the bed. Wordless, she turned and walked away.

Francine heard the sound of pots clanging in the kitchen rise through the floor. A long time later the voice of her husband spoke to their daughter

~

Michael woke soaked in sweat with no memory of how he got to be in this bed. He freed himself from the green sheet. The smell of someone who'd gone days without showering stung his nose. His eyes focused on the white walls around him, and then found a small television suspended from the ceiling just beyond the end of the bed. Chances were his activities were being recorded by it. To his left, skinny plastic vases stuffed with yellow flowers and cards that said Get Well stood on a table near a window.

A device with a doorbell lay beside him but he thought better about pressing it. He sat at the right edge of the bed and lowered his feet to the floor. As he stood, a wave of nausea punched from his belly to his throat and flooded his head. He lowered himself back to a sitting position and looked at the vacant bed beside him. A green sheet like the one that had boxed him in stretched across it. Beyond that, a doorframe minus a door led to a dimly lit hallway. Moments later, its lights exploded to bright white. Michael propelled himself up, the sick feeling gone.

eight

The gentle, illusive limbs of her unborn secret poked from inside her belly, butterflies searching for escape. She loved the flickers. They filled her with love and a sense of protectiveness.

Keeping the life growing in her from her parents kept her in a dream without an ending. But if Darren knew, the story would become real. She'd have to tell him. After the day's last class, she caught him alone in the locker room. His eyes stormed over, and he turned to walk away, but stopped in his tracks when she called his name for a second time.

He spun round to face her, his smile stretched wide. "Linda. It's good to see you."

She held her textbooks to her chest. "It is? I need to talk to you." She felt like a child making a confession.

"Can it wait? Let's do this later." Darren tapped her shoulder.

Linda pulled away from his hand. "There's something you should know about us."

"Us? I don't belong to anyone's us."

A sting pierced Linda's throat and shot up to hide behind her eyes.

Darren watched the slow escape of her tears like he was counting them one by one. "You know I love you. Made you happy last time we got together." He laughed. "We'll do it again. Just can't be now."

"I think I might..." She searched his eyes then averted her gaze.

"Shit. Are you trying to pin something on me? If you are, I'll tell everyone who you got naked for and exactly what you did." Darren cocked his head to the side. "Your brother is creepy."

"Why are you doing this?" A thin line of snot trickled to her lips.

"Look Babes. Don't cry. Do what the other girls do. Take care of your little problem on your own." He cupped his hand under her chin, and pressed his open palm against her cheek. "If you can't do that, get back to me."

She held fast to her rage. He left her standing alone. She looked down to her belly.

Dear Diary,
He won't love our secret.

~

Months earlier James bought Francine a used Pony, white with a black interior. She'd turned the ignition twice since he handed her the keys. Other than the few times Linda borrowed it to drive her friends around, it stayed in the garage.

Francine held tight to the steering wheel. The wipers sloshed back and forth, sending wet snow flying from the windshield. She'd rehearsed the route in her head before leaving home. Not because she couldn't find her way, but because she wanted to avoid last second lane changes. The roads were slick, but the early morning traffic light. She got away with driving slowly.

The parking attendant's friendliness surprised her. She walked toward the hospital's entrance. Official visiting hours wouldn't start for close to an hour, but she counted on the nurses pretending they didn't see her sneak into her son's room. On her first visits, the drugs prevented Michael from knowing who she was. Still, she'd spent all day by his side. And as late into the evening as staff would allow.

Once she arrived to find him awake. That was the morning he began to register bits and pieces of reality and got up looking for answers. She was late. James blew up at her before she left, and took a long time convincing her he was sorry. After the tears, she accepted his ride to the hospital. When he picked her up to bring her home, she apologized for the fight.

This morning she found Michael lying in bed looking at the ceiling. He stared blankly, like he had checked out. She knew something was there.

"Honey?" Francine moved to the end of the bed, and caught his eye. "How did you sleep?"

Michael barely moved his lips but spoke coherently. His words strung together in sentences that made sense. At least she thought she understood them. Mostly he asked questions, as though he'd been away for a long time and wanted to catch up. Partly, he seemed to want to reassure himself he was awake.

The eyes that watched him were now attached to real people. He described them in accurate detail, convincing Francine he made the connection.

She reached out to him. He rolled over in the bed, his back turned to her. "I'm supposed to eat at seven. Tell her I don't want to. I get sick when she forces me."

"Michael, it's your choice whether or not you eat. You tell the nurse you're not hungry or I'll tell her."

Michael turned and gave her one of those mothers are annoying looks, something Francine hadn't seen in a while. She smiled.

"She spoon feeds me. The one with the round dark brown eyes, purple lids, straight eyelashes." Francine made a face to indicate she wasn't following.

"The one with the brown mole just by the corner of her left eye?"

She pretended to catch on, to know the nurse, had seen so many, but not this one. "I'll talk to her. And bring something for you from the cafeteria when it's open."

Michael returned to staring at the ceiling as though his mind needed to shut down. Her instincts told her to let it be.

Moments later, the nurse Michael described entered the room. A scowl pulled down her chin. "Your breakfast will be here soon dear. This time I expect you to eat. Morning, how are you, another cold one. You should sit up. I'll be around for the next nine hours. Call when you need me." She adjusted the bed, checked the charts, and paused to look at Francine. "You must be Michael's mother. I'm Mags. He tells me about you."

Francine looked to Michael. He shrugged his shoulders.

"He told me about your beautiful face, and how devastated he is about starting the fire."

Francine swallowed and tried to mask her hurt. He'd confided in this abrasive woman.

"Scarred for life. A miracle you survived. Thank God."

"Yes." Francine's eyes met with Michael's. "I'm grateful for my family."

Mags pursed her lips. "Michael is a decent kid, you really should see he eats. Give me a buzz if you need me." The nurse's rubber-soled white shoes squeaked their way out of the room.

Michael gave Francine pleading eyes. "My friend Lee was here this morning. Find her." He rolled over and passed out like he was never there with her.

～

Linda headed down the hall from one class to the next. Things went dark and unsteady in front of her. Something wet and warm gushed between her legs. She slipped into the washroom, hobbled past the girls lined up at the mirrors, and found sanctuary in the cubicle furthest from the door.

She sat on the bowl like a prisoner chained. And stared in disbelief at the shock of red on her panties. Clots expelled themselves one after another, tiny fish splashing in water. The ache in her belly became a vice gripping her genitals and lower back.

Linda drew in sharp, quick breaths. She loved this new life inside her more than anything. But her body betrayed her, worked to dispose of the baby.

A lonely, panicky feeling swept through her. Crying and gagging became one sensation. She cupped her hands between her legs and caught the perfect, still, blue fetus. Mesmerized, she memorized the little girl in her hands through a wet blur.

All sounds but that of her breathing left the room. She placed the baby over her legs, and unbuttoned her sweater. Gently wrapped the lifeless body in it, and placed the bundle on the toilet shelf. She wiped herself, and pulled up her pants.

Linda walked down the hall cradling her swaddled baby. She left the school without her jacket, and found the nearest bus stop. Boarded a bus that would take her to the hospital, the same place her mother had stayed after the fire, the same place her brother now spent his days and nights.

The bus dropped her off in front of the brick building. She walked a straight path through the snow to the emergency entrance. Her eyes begged with the admissions receptionist's. "My baby died." Linda dropped to the floor. She reached out to the small package beside her.

~

James drove up the driveway to a dark house. The time was nine-thirty, early for his girls to be in bed. He fumbled with the key in the lock, swung open the door, and let panic overtake his annoyance.

A quick check of every room revealed an empty house. No sign of anyone having been in it since he left that morning. Francine might be late coming home from the hospital. He'd worry about her later. Linda should've returned from school. Made supper for the two of them. Started in on the laundry.

He hated himself for where he'd gone after work, for what he'd done with Dorothy, for leaving his daughter alone. He left every light on in the house, got back in the car, and drove to the hospital. If he could catch Francine, she might know what to do and where to find Linda.

He knew he was wrong to visit his son only those few times. Francine didn't understand the torture he felt seeing Michael sprawled on his back. When he wasn't wiggling like a worm cut in half, he was a zombie in chains.

James hurried down the hospital corridor. As he approached the bed, Michael's half-open lids slid closed. Francine was looking out the window.

James touched her shoulder from behind. "Fran." His voice matched the room's subdued lighting. "Linda didn't make it home yet."

Francine turned around, her eyes swollen. "She's here James." She looked at him like she wished she could take back her words.

James put his arms around her, and drew her head to his shoulder. "Things will be alright Baby, Linda's here? In the cafeteria?"

Francine shook her head. She sobbed into his shirt.

"Christ's sakes, what's going on?" James took a step back, his voice an angry whisper. "Where's our daughter?"

"Here. She's been admitted overnight. She had a miscarriage.

"Why didn't you call me? Why aren't you with her?"

～

The medication they pushed on Michael's tongue during his stay gradually sent new messages, apparently not delusions. The pills said he was damaged and should get out of this life.

Finally he was allowed home. Nights, he stayed awake to the sounds of Linda's crying permeating his bedroom wall. Mornings, he lay on his back and stared at the ceiling. Afternoons, he met with the psychiatrist, Monday to Thursday - one-thirty, and Fridays - two-thirty.

The length of the doctor's white lab coat accentuated his limbs. He always wore one of two shirts under it, pink or yellow, always the same bow tie, red with green dots, sitting proudly at the wide collars. When Michael entered the office he thought of cartoons and mad scientists.

Dr. Ekwueme's pupils hid in his shiny black eyes. Fluorescent lighting overhead hit them and echoed back. The words coming from behind his crooked teeth were English, but floated between them in an accent unfamiliar to Michael.

He could barely pronounce the doctor's name. And had no memory of telling him what he seemed to already know. When he brought up Darren, Michael crammed his thoughts into the back corner of his mind and looked out the window. The last snow disappeared weeks before. Melted by a thousand flaming eyes, sparks flying when the bravest dared to escape.

The psychiatrist asked Michael how fire burns without fuel. Dared him to make a connection between the loss of his first home and his obsession. Asked why the eyes were detached and watched only him. Why they demanded he set fire to the people he loved.

Michael was alone in this. The family therapy had been put on hold weeks ago. Barely one sentence worth of words were spoken the first session. At the second, the doctor suggested they were wasting time and insisted his questions be answered.

His father's response came at a volume people outside the room heard. A receptionist poked her head through the door and asked if she should call security. Michael absorbed the humiliation on his mother's face. Linda left the room. When she returned, Michael was struck by the grey of her skin. Just as she walked to the chair, her body toppled to the floor. After she came to, the session was canceled.

Michael followed the wave of Dr. Ekwueme's hand in front of his face.

The doctor snapped two long fingers. "You know, I lived in a village before I arrived in Canada. As a child I learned to treat fire with reverence, respect. What do you think about that?"

"Doctor, I'm sorry for what I've done. Already told you that."

"I believe you."

"Can we stop now?"

"Do you feel prepared to go back to your studies?"

"No." Michael slumped in his chair. "My dad says I have to."

"It's not your father who must cope with your illness Michael."

Michael dropped his face into his hands and told himself to shut-up.

~

Darren walked though the 7-Eleven doors and caught him from the periphery of his vision. He got in line and watched from behind as he paid for a pack of smokes. The wool coat on his back said money. Darren cleared his throat and the man turned to look.

"Mr. Ballantine? Darren extended his hand.
"Uh huh?"
"Remember? Darren Amsel. We were neighbours?"
"Of course. I hear your mom is sick."
"It's her brain. She's on radiation. The doctors say the tumour is shrinking."
"Hope she'll be okay."
Darren took a sideways step toward the exit. "Say hi to Michael and Linda for me?"
"I'll do that."

~

Things were quiet, and sadness washed over Linda. She looked in the mirror and saw a mother who failed her child.

Michael had been kept in the dark, and that left her free to be there for him. July and August she spent one hazy day after another coaxing him out of his room, out of the house, into the world.

She started small. Walks to 7-Eleven for Slurpees. They sat drinking them on a bench in the playground behind their place. He complained of the heat, said the pills made his skin itch. Most days he returned to his room before they could get to the bottom of their cups.

One afternoon she dragged him to a movie downtown. They sat in the center of the theater, crowded by waves of wiggles, popcorn crunch, and soda slurp. She studied his reaction to the story onscreen. Hoped to see his expression freed from its blank stare. *Willy Wonka* gave her glimpses of a timid smile. The little brother she knew.

On the bus ride home, Michael suggested they get off one stop sooner and pick up a bag of penny candy. She watched him consider his choices, and believed she could heal him with kindness.

Keeping Michael occupied worked to stop her parents from losing it. Linda would make them a whole family. Saturday morning, she got out of bed early, packed a basket of food she insisted they eat at the backyard picnic table. Slices of white bread, crusts trimmed, topped with thick luncheon meats, slices of cheese and tomatoes. A crystal bowl of dill pickle spears, pimento stuffed olives, carrot and celery sticks.

Under the kind sun, the muscles in her dad's face loosened their hold. He told stories of goofy things his builders did. Hammer throwing contests, pranks involving two by fours. Her mom laughed from under the straw hat shading her face, stole glances of Michael, his face lit by talk of home design.

Linda set aside her pain. Returned to it when she lay in bed at night. So no one would hear her grief, she crammed a pillowcase corner in her mouth. She wished she could tell Michael. But couldn't hurt her little brother.

Dear Diary,

Turned inside out. Every raw thing exposed. Been thinking of a way to say how it feels to lose a child. Can't do it with words. Darren doesn't know how special she'd be.

nine

Summer passed. Michael returned to school. The voices returned to him. He wasn't as sure they were real. When whispers came from around the hall corners, he moved in close to verify their status. They were different than those that spoke before the medication. Shot like caps from a gun.

"Fire, fire, fire, fire."

Michael stopped just before the edge where the two walls met. Crouched down, he spread his fingers spider-like on the floor. He stretched out his neck and peeked down the hall that led to the library. Muffled sounds of exchanged laughter drifted from the boy's washroom halfway down.

A school secretary put her hand on his shoulder from behind. He jerked and slipped on the green tiles. She bent over and reached out her hand. He stared at the brown-flecked eyes reflecting his confusion.

All he could do was mumble an excuse about looking for something. He scrambled up, ran to the washroom, and slammed the door behind him. The sound of his heart beating bounced off the white cement walls. One by one he opened the doors to three empty stalls.

An expressionless face judged him from the mirror. Some time passed before he realized it was his own. A long time later a grade seven kid walked in and threw his textbook in the sink. At first, he didn't seem to notice Michael, and then stopped short of the urinal, cranked his neck around, and opened his eyes wide. Michael looked into the sink and wished he could hide in its drain. He turned on the tap and rubbed his hands under icy water. The boy snatched up his book and took quick steps to the door.

The school whispers accelerated over the weeks. Michael resigned himself to them like a nail to a hammer. Not the fact they spoke to him, but that they saved their campaign for the halls made him suspicious.

The voices before his medication never said sick things about Linda. Liars. He wouldn't do that to her or anyone else. The voices before the pills didn't laugh the same way. Sometimes these giggled like girls. Other times they threw out curses out like guys who thought they were cool.

~

Darren was behind the lies. Those who'd never noticed Linda before made silent eye contact as they passed her in the hall. Some looked at her with disgust, others pity. Few spoke to her.

As the talk stretched its arms, Linda's world shrank to a box of self-hatred. She bought a pack of Bic lighters as ammunition against it. Like he thought it funny, the big-bellied man behind the 7-Eleven counter slapped a pack of cigarettes beside the cellophane bag of plastic cylinders. She paid for them both, but left the cigarettes behind.

For a week the unopened package hid with her diary. On a Sunday morning, she tore it open and spilled the red, green, and yellow lighters on her bed. She held one in her right hand and surveyed the inside crook of her left arm, its skin soft and innocent. Flicking her thumb on the roller, she held the flame against her skin. The pain, punishment for the day her body expelled her baby. Though she didn't understand why, the act of hurting herself made her feel she and Darren were still connected to each other.

Bending her arm shut, she imprisoned the angry burn. Unfolding her arm and biting her tongue, she set the flame to the same place. Cold tears fell without permission. She wished she could send them back. Her baby girl never knew what it was to cry.

The bandages were kept in a drawer in the washroom. The wound took two strips placed side by side. She pulled her cotton nightgown sleeve over them, and stashed the lighters in a zippered pocket of her shoulder bag. Linda felt more at peace than she had in weeks. Five minutes later she headed downstairs to make brunch for her family.

~

Her dad soaked up the yolk with the piece of pancake at the end of his fork. He smiled at Linda and pushed his plate forward. "Thanks for breakfast."

Linda smiled, lowered her lids. She could've done better, the toast burnt at its edges.

"I echo your father's sentiments." Her mom stood. Gathering the four empty plates, she stacked them, and balanced four glasses on top of them. She looked at Michael as he rose from his chair.

He walked around the oval table, collecting the cutlery and mugs inside an empty juice pitcher, and placed it in the sink. He ran the tap water full blast over a glob of dish soap. A mass of bubbles spilled out of the sink and on the counter.

Her mom put her hand on Michael's back. "You go ahead. I'll look after the dishes."

Her dad pushed back his chair. "I'd love to spend more time here, but I've got business to take care of."

Her mom stepped closer to the counter, and faced the sink. She sponged a plate, shook it, and banged it into a slot of the open dishwasher.

Arms dangling at her side, Linda leaned against the counter beside her.

"I'm sure your mother wouldn't mind some help." Her dad walked up behind her mom, put his hands around her waist, and burrowed his nose into her neck.

She tilted her head against his nuzzle. "Stop tickling me." Her hands in the water, she swished the bubbles in a figure eight.

"Did you hear that? Your mother wants me to stop." He laughed.

"Just go." Her mom swung around to see him leave the room.

As he shut the front door behind him, Linda slunk up the stairs. The plastic yellow lighter hidden inside her bag waited to sing harmony to her self-hatred.

~

A cold blue filtered through the living room sheers. The last two weeks of winter mornings showed no mercy, lighting everything for what it was. A layer of dust veiled the two end tables and the shaded lamps that sat on them. The record albums sat neglected in a staggered stack on top of the stereo. And the unfinished painting on the easel in front of Francine refused to yield itself to her imagination.

The irises, meant to evoke bravery, cowered under an impassive tree. A dull grape satirized the indigo she envisioned saturating their petals. The mud they sat mired in not the rich forest floor she hoped for. The only thing she managed to capture was a sense of being trapped. She wanted to dig out the flowers, transplant them to a place they'd thrive.

Francine squeezed dabs of Prussian Blue and Naphthol Crimson side by side on the wood palette. Mixing the two produced a purple that triggered a memory. It came fast, and it was hard to know whether it was real.

Francine awakes to a scream. She tiptoes downstairs to find her mother standing alone in the dark kitchen. She mumbles things about conspiring with the devil. Her mother looks at her with the eyes of a stranger, glues her bare feet to the floor when Francine tries to lead her back to bed. Her father comes from outside wearing a trench coat, a spade in one hand, a bunch of irises in the other. Her mother falls to her knees. The spade and the flowers drop from her father's hands.

Francine has the chubby arms of a preschool child and wears a long white nightgown. Her hair is tied back with a strip of white cotton. She puts a thumb in her mouth and watches in disbelief.

The image of herself as a child cast a shadow on the way she remembered her mother's spells. Francine left the easel, roamed the upstairs, replaying the memory until she felt a pull to Michael's room. The mid-morning light had transformed from grey to translucent silver. She pulled a stack of papers from the bottom drawer of his desk and tapped them into alignment on its surface. Laying them flat, her eyes rested on a detailed blueprint done in Michael's hand. She sat in the chair, examining it, and all those beneath.

Michael had created twenty-one original home designs. The work of a gifted architect spoke from every page. She wondered whether he copied them. But the plans were too personal. Each held an unusual amount of exits. She deciphered the symbol key. Escape routes, secret tunnels, hatches.

Dear Diary,

Mom's eyes are as beautiful as they were before the fire. The person she used to be speaks through them. She doesn't know, but I do.

They were nothing. But he owned them. Darren amazed himself, so easy to bring down two at once. Michael and Linda both.

Next he'd deal with his old man. Like he'd call him that to his face. Sieg heil prick. Make sure he never beat him again. Have his friend Hitler march him to the ovens. Watch his body fly away in smoke and flakes. Bye bye Papa.

Mama would follow behind. Like in real life. He was sick of her acting like he was a mistake. Because he saw the truth, he shamed her.

He had no memory of his father saying a kind word. The closest his mother came was when she thought she might die. "Darling, you must understand I only want what is best for you." When the doctors said there was a chance she'd make it, Darren returned to worthless; she to molding him into a freak. For long stretches he'd let her believe she was winning, then to piss her off, showed her his ugly insides. He lived for the look on her face when she realized he'd duped her. Trapped like a stupid rabbit.

Traps. Fires. They fascinated him, a bigger rush than convincing some chick to spread her legs. Traps because they made him king. Fires because kings destroy.

~

Before she realized whom it belonged to, the hand on her shoulder sent waves to her center. No one had touched her in weeks. Linda's eyes locked with his steel grey. She searched for a soul inside. Lips parted in confusion, she looked down. Darren squeezed her shoulder. She did nothing to stop him. He took her hand in his.

She lifted her eyes to meet his again. "Darren. Why are you doing this?"

"That's what I wanna talk to you about. I want us to start over."

Linda looked down the hall at a group of girls standing in a circle. "I don't want people to see us."

"We got a lot to talk about. I get it. I'll give you what you need. Promise."

"No one should forgive what you've done."

"I need help. Doesn't mean I don't love you. I can do it for you."

"Do what?" Her fingers brushed against the hand on her shoulder as if to remove it, but rested there instead.

Darren took in a breath. "I love you. I'm sorry."

The sound of approaching footsteps untangled them. Darren walked away, and then turned around. "Meet me behind the school last class." He whisked down the hall.

Thursday night, his mother laid out a Sunday meal - roast beef, potatoes, gravy, green beans, and tapioca pudding. No one acknowledged the menu change.

Michael sat across the kitchen table from his sister. The colour of her skin seemed paler than the day before, the blue under her eyes, darker. He thought of getting up and hugging her. But that would be too much. He stayed in his chair.

Michael remembered sitting with his family in the Creekwater Bay kitchen. They gobbled mounds of crusty-top macaroni. Linda chattered on about how she and her friends planned to put on a puppet show the next afternoon. The two cents in advance fee would buy Kool-Aid, crackers, and pretzels for a concession table. Linda turned to Michael with sparkling eyes and asked if he'd help collect the money. They'd go door to door. She was his world, his enthusiasm a bubble popping from a wand.

Linda sank in her chair and wrapped her arms around herself.

Michael leaned forward. "I have something to show you Dad. After supper." He stirred his pudding. "And you too Linda."

She answered from a place far away. "What's this about?"

"I drew up some plans."

James felt a pride he hadn't for a long time. His son had talent. The blueprints frayed at the edges, but their quality and innovation rose above many he'd seen, a pinprick of hope. Michael may have faced his demons.

James thought he might show the work to his colleagues. Anyone could see the inspiration. His son may have opened the door to the future.

Linda spoke to James as though Michael weren't there. She pointed to the outlines of the paths inside the layouts. If she walked through each house room to room, starting from the front doors and eventually to the back, her feet would trace a series of triangles.

"That's some impressive work you've done." James placed his hand on Michael's shoulder. "Apart from the underground tunnels and hidden doorways." He chuckled like the two were sharing an inside joke. "I see the number of windows you've got going here; their shapes could become popular." James tapped the back of his right hand on the stack of papers.

Linda's big sister smile broke through. She winked at Michael. "You always had a cool imagination. You should keep using it."

~

Francine loaded the dishwasher, and then tackled the roasting pan with a steel wool scrubber. The people she loved were upstairs and happy in each other's company. Exactly what made these moments happen, she didn't know. They were spontaneous gifts. Long stretches went between this magic.

Sweeping the floor, she listened to the sounds of her family through the kitchen ceiling. She tapped the dustpan into the garbage tin kept in the cupboard under the sink and stashed it, along with the broom, into the closet. James met her at the bottom of the stairs. Linda and Michael followed behind.

"Let's sit awhile." Francine's hand pointed to the living room.

"I don't see why not." James drew Francine close and kissed her forehead.

～

Michael sat at his desk, the blueprints spread on top. He studied them one at a time. They spoke to him like friends. Not like the voices that bullied him.

He needed to know where those came from. Some exploded in his mind like nightmares. Others came from outside his head. Like those he heard in school.

Michael and his sister may have been stuffed in two separate jail cells, but he'd pry his way loose for the both of them. Someone had to stop her. Darren couldn't.

Michael pulled himself away from his desk and plopped on top of his bed. He wished he didn't know what he did. *Dear Diary.* His revved up thinking kept him from closing his eyes.

ten

Michael planned to catch the voices in the act, but needed back up. The only guy who had the heart was George.

"Your eyes. They jitter like golf sockets." He tilted his head to the left, and then the right.

The theatrics gave Michael hope. "Why do you talk like that?"

George's lopsided smile said they were tight. "You got me. But where have you been? For long hours I have missed the benefit of your company."

Michael gently pressed his fist against his friend's chest.

George wrapped his hand around it. "Come by my place this weekend. Brother number two wrote some lyrics. When I sing them, my voice is butter on your crumpet."

"Yeah?"

The look on his face said George was puzzled. "There's something of import you wish to impart? You look like a serious skeleton."

The first few words came out in a stutter. "I need you to do something for me." Michael got the next words out in a hurry. "I've been hearing voices in the hall. I'm sure they're real."

George's eyes swung to the ceiling, then to his shuffling feet. A long silence passed. "The voices are real." George reached out, wrapped his arms around him, and then gently held him at arm's length.

Michael stepped back and crossed his hands in a martial arts pose. "What's that aftershave you're wearing?"

George made a chopping motion with his right hand. "Be careful how you use it." His tone deepened. "Whatever you need. I will be of your assistance."

Michael exhaled. "I'll come by your place Saturday."

~

The wind lifted and cried out behind the school. Darren faced the wall, took a step closer, and pressed his head into the bricks. His toque snagged against their rough surface. He looked at his watch. An hour after last class was let out. The bitch left him here to freeze his ass off.

He punched the wall. The garbage mitt on his hand gave little padding against the force of his blow. Shit. He removed it with watery eyes. The injury looked like it felt, mean and angry. He tilted his head up and let the snot clogging his nose run down his throat.

He more sensed than heard her treading towards him, swung round, and scowled. When he saw her, his expression fell away.

"Darren." Linda stopped a few feet short of where he stood.

Something was off. He considered putting his face back on. "What took you so long?"

"I thought about not showing, then changed my mind."

"So what made you come?"

Linda moved closer. "I love you. And you love me."

Darren wished there was somewhere they could go to be alone. But had no magic to make that place exist. He took her by the hand and led her toward the back entrance steps. The walls to either side cut the wind. Her arms tight around his waist, she leaned her cheek against his chest.

She was so easily conquered. But she made him special the way no one else had. He was Jesus with his bloody Mary.

The image of his own mother repulsed him. Did she ever love him? He imagined her leaving him to cry it out in his crib. The only time she touched him was with a finger stiff against his chest. "Take my advice, follow the example of your brothers, or you'll answer to your father." Darren shook his head to clear it of her voice.

Linda sobbed into his jacket. Her body shook. "I'm not alone with this anymore."

Darren patted the top of her head. "Don't cry. What happened is over."

"I had no one to talk to."

"Yeah. I heard the shit people were saying. It hurt me too."

Linda became still. Her voice lowered. "I miss our baby." She looked into his eyes. "You should've seen her."

"Don't talk to me about that." Darren wiped his dripping nose with the back of his mitt.

"She was beautiful."

Dear Diary,

Darren would have to be burned alive to understand the pain he's caused.

Four brothers and their equipment crammed into a corner of the unfinished rec room. The electric guitars buzzed along with the raw emotion in the lyrics. George sang his solo like Mick Jagger with a case of strep throat. Michael's lips drew into a smile. He felt normal again and was happy to have these guys for friends.

George's hair plastered itself in wet curls against his face. He swiped the back of his hand across his forehead. Grabbing hold of the bottom of his t-shirt, he waved it like a parachute, airing himself. "You like?"

All eyes looked at Michael. He hesitated. "Yeah, I do. Very cool."

George pounded his chest with his fist. "Far out. Now Michael, who towers over me, let us retire to the next room where we can discuss your persecution."

Michael sighed, and then shook his head. "The way you talk."

George had been given first choice of bedrooms, but chose a corner of the basement instead. He built walls with stacks of books. As he sampled one or two, the walls were rearranged. A stash of record albums lay on top of his bed. He moved some to the side, and then motioned for Michael to sit down beside him.

George picked up one of the albums and held it on his lap. "I love the cover art."

Michael studied it. The album's title was doodled with fat, cute letters. The innocence of the graphics gave no hint of the messages contained within.

Michael pulled the album from George's hands. "I like it too. I'm the one who gave it to you, remember?"

George grabbed it back. "Want to listen to it?" He stood up and shouted over a wall of books. "Hey brothers, shut-up the jam session. Michael wants to hear some good music."

Their playing stopped mid-song, then started up quietly. The snare drum cut through as George lowered the needle arm to the record.

The vocals made Michael sad, sung by a rocker ghost, like Janis Joplin.

George twirled the end of a curl around his finger. "The new lead is no match for the original, but both have groovy tresses."

"I like him anyway." Michael interlaced his fingers.

George did the same with his. "You dig this tune because you know what it feels like to be a victim."

"What are you talking about? What do you know?" Michael words came out fast.

"I know what has been done and who has been doing it." George leaned toward Michael. "I'm sorry for not stepping in."

"What? Who?"

"Someone has to stop your sister from playing with fire."

∼

Linda and Darren sat at a long table in the downtown public library, their chairs turned face-to-face. Linda chose it as their meeting place. Other than an elderly man wandering the Philosophy section, the second floor was deserted.

"Darren." Linda tucked his hair behind his ears. "Why do you think I keep you a secret?"

"Because it turns you on?"

Linda pretended to smack Darren's cheek, and then patted it. He put his hand over hers.

Darren whispered, "Let's go somewhere."

Linda raised her other hand to his face. "We are somewhere. Where do you want to go?"

"Don't know. I don't care."

Linda's eyes followed the smallest movements of his. "I see you do Darren. But I'm not ready." She lowered her hands to her lap, studied them as she spoke.

"It's what you need." Darren moved close, pressed his lips against hers, wedged his hand between her knees.

Linda pulled away. "What are you doing? Maybe I don't want to forget."

"I'm not giving up." Darren smiled, leaned forward in his chair, and kissed her forehead.

"Whatever you have planned can't happen."

"You have no idea what you're missing." Darren rested his hands on her shoulders. "Please?"

"You're funny." She nodded toward the white-haired man emerging from the long aisle of books. "No Darren."

Darren picked up a pen and scribbled something on the cover of a Vogue magazine lying on the table.

"I take it back. You're not funny." Linda rose from her seat and picked up the jacket draped over its back. "Let's go."

They spent the rest of the morning holding hands and wandering the streets downtown. Linda made a game of finding outdated signs. Darren claimed the oldest was a Pepsi ad painted on the side of the St. Charles Hotel. Linda said a brick building next to a steepled church held one older, but couldn't remember where it was.

When the cold became too much, they slipped in and out of the stores along Portage Avenue - Mother's Music, The Chocolate Shop, Orientique, Solar News. Darren begged Linda to make their last stop Long John Silver's. He wanted to squeeze in some pool. She glued her back to a wall in the dark basement room, choked on the cigarette smoke, and watched Darren try to hustle a boy too young to be there. But who won the game.

Linda headed to the washroom before they left. Darren didn't notice her return. She saw him offer the kid a cigarette like he was giving him a prize. Then he slipped a black and silver striped case in his jacket's inside pocket. He turned to Linda and froze, like he'd been caught. "Hey don't sneak up on me like that."

The ride home was quiet, the bus almost empty. Linda watched the buildings pass. Darren kept his eyes closed, sat upright in the seat across the aisle from her. The driver smoked a cigarette, holding it out the open window between drags.

~

George grabbed the back of Michael's jacket and pulled him to the floor. "Duck."

To keep from falling, Michael spread his fingers on the gold-flecked carpet.

George stretched his neck over the row of record albums. "There they are." He put a finger to his lips.

Michael smirked.

George scowled. "Why the need to scoff at me? Look for yourself."

Michael's heart chugged like a cold motor struggling to turn over. Linda and Darren had their backs turned to them. They stood side by side looking at the album in Darren's hands. Linda elbowed him in the waist and laughed. Darren sang something to her, or Michael was imagining things.

George whispered. "I don't take pleasure in having to show you this." He gestured at Michael for them to leave the store.

A bell tinkled as the door closed behind them. On the sidewalk in front of the store, George pulled Michael away from the window. Heads lowered against the wind, they walked down Portage Avenue toward Main Street.

Michel shoved his hands in his pockets. "Do you think they saw us?"

"Almost certain they did not. Put your hood up in disguise. You can't be sure about Darren."

"We have to warn her, before something happens."

"I am sorry to report the futility in that."

"What do you mean?"

George steered Michael toward Garry Street. "We'll eat lunch down here."

~

The waitress placed two baskets side-by-side on the table. Lined with checkered tea towels, they spilled over with fries and breaded chicken strips.

Michael leaned across the table toward George. "Tell me what's going on and don't make me wait until you're done eating all that."

George picked up the tall cup in front of him and took a long drag through the paper straw. He placed it down and his fingertips vanished from the frosty glass.

"My friend. I don't wish to hurt you, but will tell you what people have been saying. These are not my words." George studied the tablecloth for a long time. "Darren knocked up your sister."

Michael scanned the room.

"What is it with your eyes in times of distress?" George sat back. "Focus on what I have to say. There's more."

"Linda is not pregnant." Michael got up from his chair, stormed to the washroom, and locked himself inside a stall.

Just as Michael opened the washroom door again, the waitress returned to the table and asked George what was going on. "Look. I don't need any trouble." She looked Michael up and down, turned, and walked away.

As Michael approached the table, George directed his comment at him. "Then trouble you will not get."

Michael answered with conviction. "I know the story, but I won't betray my sister. There's nothing more to say."

~

James kissed the top of her head an hour ago. Spoke softly into her hair before leaving for work. Francine turned over in their bed, bundled herself tight in the wool blankets. She drifted off and his words worked their way into a dream about an art show. Artists literally starving. She left a display of her own work to walk the aisles, row after row of strangely beautiful paintings.

The show became a maze as she tried to find her way back. When she found her work, a crowd gathered around.

Two women with missing teeth debated whether it was intended to be funny. A man in a cheap suit turned one painting upside down. The laughter he provoked shook her from the dream.

The clock radio's red lines said eight. She'd been in bed twelve hours, had no desire to get out to face another day, or herself in the mirror.

Francine forced down a bowl of oatmeal and drank some tea before she set out to paint. Though she hadn't decided, this piece might be her last. With attention to every detail, she transferred the image of herself in the mirror to the largest canvas she'd worked, a five by six foot piece of pure white. She'd create beauty from her ugliness.

Francine picked up a charcoal pencil and sketched the raised scar trailing from her neck up to her left temple, imagined a vole burrowing underground. Her eyebrows became rows of centipedes. Her hair, foxtail grasses sheltering nameless wildflowers. She imagined merging into nature. Wiped clean, her face served a practical god, a naked truth.

In faint lines, Francine completed the outlines of the contours of her head, face, and neck. She surrounded her eyes with wispy lashes, drawing those from a mix of memory and imagination. Tossing the pencil into the shoebox beside her, she considered the paints stashed inside.

The colours she chose would take her to somewhere she belonged. She lined the tubes along the edge of the kitchen table. Burnt Sienna. Viridian Hue. Phthalo Green. Dioxazine Purple. Manganese Blue. Mars Black. Raw Umber. French Ultramarine Blue. Parchment. Cadmium Yellow. Brilliant Purple. Tints that would sculpt her face.

The blood traveling through her raised veins, the scars mapping territory over blotchy terrain, her disfigured features, transformed.

~

The plan was set though all the details hadn't been worked out. George would trail Michael at school, especially when he went into the basement. George would hide behind the lockers and catch the voices in the act.

The first few days nothing much happened other than Michael and George arriving late for classes. By Thursday, Michael heard the voices. He stood alone inside a first floor side entrance intended for staff.

Someone called out Psycho Boy three times. Michael spun round looking for George. All he saw were rows of tiles down the hall and what looked like a male figure making his way across them.

Michael's brain fired emergency signals. He moved his feet a few steps forward, a few back, turned to the side, banged his palms together, chunk chunk chunk.

Turning his back to the approaching figure, Michael leaned his forehead against the glass door. The snow on the step just outside reflected back. The words he muttered made fog against the pane, "Are you? Nobody."

The hands placed on his shoulders burned to his bones. He screamed, and cowered in the corner. Protecting his head with his arms, he tried to cram himself into the floor. The hands moved to his back and rubbed up and down.

"Michael. It's George. I'll take you home."

Michael surrendered. He rose and stepped out of his shoes, holding his extended arms and wrists together as though ready to be handcuffed.

George picked up Michael's shoes and led him away from the door, around a corner, and into the staff washroom. He sat him down in a cubicle and closed the door. "Wait here. I'll get our jackets."

Michael had been locked in a small prison cell, made for the criminal he was.

~

Francine chose her brushes with the same thought she chose the tubes of paint. She lined them up beside the palette: two flats, two rounds, an angle, a filbert, and a fan. The cadmium yellow drew her first. She squeezed out a quarter-sized glob, and then pressed out a penny of Naphthol Crimson beside it. With one of the rounds, she picked up dabs of both, and considered where to begin. Just as she slid the brush onto the canvas, inside an ear and over a lobe, the doorbell rang. The person holding it refused its release.

She dropped the brush and hurried to the door. Michael's cries for help came from the other side. He screamed like a scared two year old. The open door revealed another boy, one she'd never seen, his arms locked into her son's from behind. Michael's wild eyes screamed for escape.

Francine spoke to the boy. "Bring him in."

The boy took short breaths and used his knees to push Michael through. Once inside, he unhooked his arms from under Michael's, and wrapped himself around him. Michael lowered his head into the boy's chest. Francine slammed the door and whisked the deadbolt into place.

She stood a silent witness to the heartbreaking embrace. "Help me get him to his room."

"No Mom." Michael turned to her. He made motions with his chin indicating he wanted to be released. "I'm okay."

George let go and rested his arms by his side. He followed Michael's lead, removed his winter boots, and headed for the living room sofa.

Francine sat on the loveseat across from them. She waited awhile before she spoke. "I'm Francine."

"George Jirizek, schoolmate to your son." Taking a deep breath, he looked to his hands clutching his thighs. "I'm here because Michael has known many bullies, and they are led by your daughter's friend."

"What are you saying?" Francine shook her head and moved forward as if to rise.

"Please stay with us." George waved his hand up and down. "I'm not suggesting Linda would intentionally cause Michael pain. But she has made an alliance with a person you shouldn't dismiss."

This boy spoke like someone who fought with life before his time. Francine turned to Michael. "What can you tell me about this?"

He leaned forward, put his face in his hands and muttered through his fingers. "The voices are real. They belong to real people. Darren Amsel is the one who controls them."

"I don't know what to believe." Francine moved across the room, knelt in front of her son, and stroked his hair. "Maybe the doctor can advise us."

Michael removed his mother's hand, and placed it by her side. "No. Give George a chance. He's got bad news. Something you should know."

∼

Francine called James at work, and worried he might lose it, spoke with words softened at their edges. He told her to stay calm, keep Michael and his friend the same. If the medications weren't doing their job, the psychiatrist would have to come up with something better. They had their son back for a time; they'd have him again.

She held back the picture window shears with one hand and watched for his car. The boys sat beside each other on the sofa behind her. George responded to Michael's muttering with whispers. Trapped in her own thoughts, she lost the gist of what they said. But some words stuck out. Cafeteria. Conspiracy.

James came through the front door, stood in the entrance, and stuck his head around the corner. "Son, you and I'll take a trip to Dr. Ekwueme's." He gave Francine a stern look and stuffed his gloves into his overcoat pockets.

Michael rose and headed to the door. He wedged his feet in his boots and turned to leave.

James winked at George. "Thanks for bringing him here. You've done the right thing."

George made a motion to get up, but James said not to. "Francine, get the boy something to eat."

Through the window, Francine watched James open the passenger door and then Michael slip into the car. James slammed the door shut.

∼

The side effects ate him up. Michael confessed that for weeks he stashed his pills under his tongue and spit them in the toilet. When he took them he had a few feet to step in any direction before he met with fog. They urged him to sleep and hope to never wake. The effects of being drugged wearing off, he could pay attention to what went on around him. Michael was fine, except for one thing.

"And what might that be?" Dr. Ekwueme looked up from his notepad and tapped the pen against it.

"I wish I had George with me. It's hard for me to get the words out."

"And he would be the friend who brought you to your mother. She believes you were having a psychotic break." The doctor's words came out more like questions than statements.

"George would tell you about Darren, how he wants to ruin me."

"I want to hear more, but first we discuss tinkering with your meds. As I've explained, what will or won't work is sometimes trial and error."

Michael looked at the doctor's polished, white shoes. Their elevator heels made a statement. "Medication gets in my way. I have to stop Linda from hurting Darren."

"I have other patients your age Michael. They tell me similar stories." Dr. Ekwueme reached out to a table nearby. He placed the note pad on it, and then leaned toward Michael. "What classmates do to torment students who suffer from mental illness is inexcusable. That matter needs to be addressed. But first we must make a distinction between what is real and what is not."

"Darren is real. What he does to me, unreal."

"I trust you. Trust me when I say you look thinner since we last met, worn and pale."

Michael played along; doing so would buy him time. He named the things he'd change - the pain he caused his mother, her scars, and the way his father looked at him as though he were unsure how to act. He wished he could peel off the label glued to his face.

eleven

Darren opened the back door to Linda. "Everyone's at my aunt's. Come see my room." He reached for her hand, led her through the quiet house, and stopped at the closed bedroom door. "I faked the flu to get you alone." He dropped her hand, opened the door, and walked inside.

She leaned against the door's frame. The hardwood floors shone like melting ice. A beige spread confined two thin pillows at the head of Darren's bed. He sat at its foot and patted the space beside him. "Gotta talk to you. About my dad."

They sat facing an open closet. To the far left, his shirts hung in an evenly spaced row, followed by his pants. To their right, three blazers and a wool overcoat lined up like soldiers.

"Where do you wear those dress-up clothes?" Linda tugged on Darren's earlobe.

"You wanna see me in them?" Darren lifted his eyebrows. He removed the shirt from his back and threw it to the floor.

"Tell me about your dad."

"The thing is I'm sure he's in love with you." Darren wiped away pretend tears.

Linda put her head against his shoulder and laughed.

"I'm serious."

Linda turned to Darren, pulled up her legs, and crossed them under herself. Her eyes surveyed his, and, for a moment traveled to the blank blue wall behind him. She felt herself drift.

Darren reached over to hold her hands upright in his. "We love each other."

Linda took her hands back. "We're keeping secrets. What love is that?"

"You want me to tell my dad about you?"

Linda slid her fingers over the green-tinged bruises on Darren's chest. "You should."

Darren placed his hands on his thighs. A smoky grey billowed behind his irises. "If you're not sure!"

She interrupted his sentence with a kiss to his temple. "Can we talk about this later?" Her fingertips turned his face toward hers. "You can't love me as much as I love you."

Darren kissed her lips, and pulled back. "There's something I wanna give you. Wait here." He got up and left the room.

Linda stared at the dresser beside the bed. She reached over, slid open the top drawer, and peeked inside. A corner tip of a small box poked through neatly folded clothes. She slid it out slowly and untied the string wrapped around it. After removing its contents, she retied the string, and put the box back the way it was. Wrapped in a silk handkerchief, the cigarette case easily glided into the front pocket of her jeans. She positioned herself in the same place she'd been when Darren left the room, and waited.

Dear Diary,
I found Dad's cigarette case.

Michael hadn't been able to face school in over a week. He returned to his room after breakfast and climbed into his unmade bed. He'd get ahold of George at the end of the day. The two of them could come up with another plan. A long stretch of day lay ahead first.

He drew back the curtains. A clear morning sky lit the room. He sat in the desk chair, pulled open the drawer, and laid out the stack of blueprints he created months ago. Back when his mind still held visions. He rummaged for some blank paper and set it beside the stack.

Michael hoped for a fresh start. The impression of confinement the plans conveyed inspired him to take his ideas in the opposite direction. He'd create a home where everything served a practical purpose. Simplicity and transparency would be its beauty.

He began with the front entrance. It would connect to a hallway leading to the kitchen. A circular path would connect that to the dining and living rooms. Each area would serve a separate, but inter-connected purpose, make individual statements, but flow one into the other, creating a sense of unity. The walls and doors would be structured from opaque glass blocks lit from within, the ceilings covered with polished stainless steel. Off to the side of the front entrance, a staircase would lead to a second floor holding three bedrooms and a bathroom. The bedrooms would have dressers built into the walls, bed frames that pulled up from the floor. Storage units would hide within the six surfaces of each room.

After laying down the basics, Michael sketched in the details: vents, light fixtures, outlets, and switches. Living rooms ask for an element of comfort. He penciled in a square shape on the far wall, and then held the eraser over it. He came up with a new kind of fireplace, not lit by fire, but outdoor light. Also constructed of glass, the hearth would be a large triangular window jutting into the room. Daylight sun would create a different warmth. At night incandescent flame-shaped bulbs would shine under a smaller triangle of glass at its base.

Once he completed his plan, he carefully transferred it to three more sheets of paper, and laid all four in a row to examine them. Something was missing.

His mom tapped on his door. "You've been in your room all morning. Shouldn't you come for lunch?"

Michael slipped his plans into a manila folder and put it under some magazines in the bottom drawer. His dad should see them. But not yet.

⁓

Francine flipped the grilled cheese sandwich and pressed the spatula down hard. Transferring the sandwich to a plate, she sliced it in triangles, and placed it in front of Michael.

"Can I get you something else? Juice?" Francine sat beside him at the kitchen table.

"I can get it myself."

"There must be something I can do."

Michael reached toward the plate, his eyes avoiding hers. "Take George seriously."

"And you'll do something for me?"

"Uh huh." Michael drew out the two syllables.

Francine placed her right hand on the table and moved it toward her son. "Talk to me about the fire."

Michael put his face in his hands.

Francine got up to stand beside him, and pried apart his hands. "I'm okay with who I am."

Michael hung his head. "It's not that simple."

"I know people see tragedy when they look at me, but that I'm different on the outside isn't the point. I'm different on the inside too."

"I can't forgive myself." Michael took her hand.

A long silence followed. Finally Francine broke it. "There's nothing to forgive. You were a child." She looked at Michael with protective eyes. "What's haunting you?"

"I didn't imagine the voice that told me to set the fire. I did what he told me so he'd stop hurting me. But he didn't. And now Linda wants to pay the price for me."

Francine felt a shiver, a mixture of confusion and shame at having been caught. What did he know? A tear rolled down her face and fell to the table.

Michael sat up straight. "I'll take care of it."

~

"We get to him through Linda." George adjusted the strings on his guitar. "If my hair grows two more inches, know who people will mistake me for?"

Michael smoothed back his own hair. "Can I have your autograph?"

"Respect my aspirations or I'll leave you behind when I reach the top."

"You won't see me from under your hair." Michael pointed at the shoes on his friend's feet. "You'll trip all over the stage in those platforms."

George shook his head from side to side, setting his curls bouncing. "All jesting pushed off to the side, we must show Darren for who he is, and Linda the devil in his details."

"How are you going to convince her he's not who he pretends to be?"

"You must alter the way in which you ask. You must change the "are you" to "am I," and then you will have answered the first part of your question."

"How can I convince her when she's willing to give it all away?"

"Darren has robbed her. You'll retrieve and return her self-worth. Once she becomes reacquainted with it, she'll forget him."

"When do we, I mean, I, start?"

"Now would be the time to begin your journey of footprints."

George's mother stepped down the stairs to his room, called him for dinner, and invited Michael to stay as she headed back up. The family took their places at the dining room table, a steaming tureen of chicken soup placed in its center. Michael was asked to sit between Pavel and Milos. George explained that their meals begin with soup, followed by *meso* and *priloha,* meat and side dishes. Michael ate quietly, listening to a family talk to each other in a language he couldn't pretend to decipher. Yet he recognized the dynamics as if no words were spoken. They wore their roles like grandma sweaters. He caught a chafing here, an itch there, a bit of pride.

~

The coffee shop was his idea. Linda wished she were anywhere else. Michael waited for his answer with wide eyes. She wrapped her hands around the mug on the table and forced herself to look at him.

Michael chose a quiet time. They were the only two customers seated that morning; apart from a middle-aged couple hovered over some paperwork. Occasionally they looked up and called out to the waiter in another language, maybe Greek. He threw receipts their way.

Michael leafed through his wallet and pulled out a school photo of Linda. He placed it in front of her. "I wish I had a picture of mom before the fire. I was six and thought she was the most beautiful woman alive. You remind me of her."

Linda flinched.

Michael leaned forward. "What does Darren mean to you?"

"He means something to you?" Linda picked up the photo and handed it back.

"Yeah, but maybe I'm the only one who knows it."

"Are you okay? Are you making sense?"

"I plan to make sense." Michael pushed his coffee cup to the side and leaned against the booth's cushion. "Darren messed me up. And I'm gonna stop him. He won't hurt you again. And you won't hurt him."

"What are you talking about?"

"He forced me to do things I'm ashamed to say. He hurt me, made me hurt myself. And I know what he did to you."

"What? Are you hearing voices?"

"I gotta tell you something."

Anger flooded Linda's face. She slid out of the booth and headed for the exit. Michael let her go.

~

Francine washed a diluted purple over the viscous green on the canvas and set her brush down. The eyes in front of her pleaded to be free. The lips parted to steal a breath. She felt a chill and gasped.

Picking up the brush, she scrubbed in a Viridian hue, setting the shadows apart from the light. With another, she stroked the curved lines with Manganese blue, and the crevices with Raw umber.

A tube of crimson and of yellow still sat on the easel's lip where she set them the morning. Michael's friend dragged him home. She'd mix the colours in various proportions and also allow each to stand alone.

The painting told a story about the will to be. She spent over two hours laying one colour over another, stepped back and realized what she'd done. She could keep this work from James. Protect him from her scars.

~

Sunday morning before church. Halfway through shoveling the driveway, James felt a stab to his ribcage. He rested the shovel against the chain link fence and stood still until it went away. Then lit a cigarette. His doctor warned him to quit. But that would be letting go of a friend. He took five drags and threw the butt into the snow.

God's fist punched him in the chest. His knees buckled and he fell forward. Frozen hell. Strangely, just before she rolled him on his back, he saw Francine's face in the white. He looked up to her bare legs buried to the hem of her nightgown. Her mouth moved as if in a silent howl.

A siren cried from far away. It took a long time to arrive, as though something held it back, and when it did, burst into a scream before it stopped dead.

∼

"If you believe him, I don't know how to change your mind. Why do you fall for Michael's shit? You're too good for that." Darren wiped the wet seeping from his nose on the back of his mitt.

"I love my brother. I'd do anything for him. Even let you go." Linda removed Darren's toque and smoothed his hair down the sides of his face. "Michael believes you're the voice he hears in his head. He needs to know you won't go near him."

"We've been secret a long time. He doesn't have to know." The hands on his face made him think of puking. He pulled away, turned toward the red brick of the school wall, kicked it, and slid down to his knees on the cement steps.

"Look at me." Linda bent down and kissed his forehead.

The back entrance to the school was the place that held their secrets and lies. Linda was the one he could say anything to. She made him important.

Darren made his tears stop. "Let me see that letter again." He extended his hand and waved his fingers. "It's mental talk. Doing what he says won't cure him." He shoved a shoulder against the wall.

Linda sat beside him. She pulled a folded piece of loose leaf from her jacket pocket and put it in his hand.

Darren clutched at the paper's edges and gave it a shake. "Listen to this mess." He read aloud. "I'll come home when Linda says she'll get rid of Darren. That's the only way.

Hope you forgive me. I'll deal with him myself. Because I love you. Please don't... " Darren handed back the paper. "I'm not gonna finish this."

⁓

Francine returned to check up on the kids. Linda greeted her at the door with a note in her hand.

"Please don't be upset. Everything will work out. I'll take care of it. You take care of Dad."

Francine had no choice other than to rely on her. After a short while, she returned to the hospital to sit beside her husband. He'd been admitted for observation, and would stay a few days. She'd wait to tell him about Michael's disappearance. Give Linda time.

Sleeping on his side, James looked almost peaceful. His head sunk in the pillow with gratitude and his arms pointed at her as though expecting an embrace. Every so often, his lips almost formed a smile.

Francine hunched forward. She felt the blood drain from her face. Her wet eyes melted into the swollen skin surrounding them and her mind was too numb to form a thought. Clumps of hair stuck to her head as they had when she got out of bed that morning and looked out the window to see James swallowed by a snow bank.

The doctor said he would recover, but that guarantee didn't hold for a next time. He'd have to comply with his orders. When did he ever bend to the will of another?

And Michael? There'd be no recovery, just reprieves. If only she could reclaim the gentle son who loved his family to a fault, if she hadn't failed as a mother and a human being.

Misplaced meaning. Like he could find it somewhere. Replace it with another. Attaching the bizarre to the ordinary. That's how the psychiatrist explained psychosis to Michael. The idea made him want to punch walls.

Now he sat watching homeless men watching him. There had to be meaning there. Some had eyes as menacing as Darren's. Others refused to be read at all, harsh men, lost men surviving the night.

The bus depot provided a place for them to sit awhile before security shuffled them out. No one questioned what Michael was doing there. He looked like a kid who belonged to someone.

The doctor tried to convince him, but Michael refused to believe his fears were based in paranoia. He had to make everyone see the hard way.

A man wearing a torn trench coat approached Michael. How could he say no to the grimy man asking for spare change? Michael handed over a few quarters. He had more stashed in his jacket pocket, and got up in search of a pay phone. He inserted the coins into the pay phone slot and closed his eyes tight. Hoped his mother would answer the phone and not Linda.

"Mom? How's Dad?"

"Michael. He needs you. We'll all be okay when you get home. Tell me where you are. I'll come get you."

"Mom. I called to let you know I'm okay. Did Linda talk to Darren?"

"I just got home from the hospital. I'm going back soon. Can you meet me there?"

"Tell Dad I love him."

"He loves you too. I love you. Linda loves you. Please come home."

"Gotta go. I'll call back."

"When Michael?"

"Bye Mom."

~

Linda left late for school. The only words she said before walking out the door were, "I love you." Almost too quiet. The breakfast Francine set out sat untouched on the kitchen table.

Francine walked into the living room. James lay propped on pillows on the sofa. He watched the morning news show without expression. She asked how he felt and he answered with how did she expect him to feel. Considering his wife kept things about his kids from him. And his heart was making plans to pack it in without his consent.

Francine said nothing and turned away. She gathered her painting supplies. Set up her easel like today was any other and turned it toward James.

"Christ Francine. Our son is missing; you insist we don't call the cops. Our family is going to hell, and you want me to watch you play with your pretty paint set."

Francine set a stool in front of the canvas and picked up a brush. "Have faith in the children. They'll work things out." She dipped into the dabs on the palette.

Concentrating on the scars, she etched them in deep with a mixture of red, brown, and green. They pulsed from beneath, not to escape, but to stake their claim. No amount of subsequent layering would hide their jagged lines.

After a long time, Francine turned to her husband. His head nodded as he fell asleep. She got up to switch off the television and kiss his forehead.

～

Two days after Michael went missing, Linda found George wandering the aisles in the school library. He carried a stack of books in his arms and insisted on checking them out before they spoke. Rather than stash the books when he retrieved his jacket from his locker, he brought them along.

"What's so important that you can't leave them behind? Linda looked at him head on. "I need you to help me find Michael."

George glanced at the stack in his hands. "My father says books are more precious than gold. I am doing the prudent thing, investing in my future, making a deposit in my heart's savings account, so that my interest might accumulate."

Linda let out a tiny puff of air. "Are you sure you know where to find him? Has he told you something I don't know?"

"One can never be certain of anything, sister to the best friend I have known. But if you place faith in my intuition, I believe I can both find and convince him to reunite with his family." The volume of George's voice built to a crescendo halfway through, and then just as gradually decreased, stopping with the precision of a musical phrase.

A short time later, they stood waiting for a downtown bus.

"Let me see that note again." George held the books toward Linda. She retrieved the folded paper from her pocket and traded with him.

George examined the spiral of words at the bottom of the page. *House on fire.* The phrase repeated and looped like the outline of a malleable dwelling, and then pointed up, the psychedelic blueprint of something only Michael could envision.

"I am certain Michael means figuratively. Not literally." George turned the drawing around and around. "The configuration of the note itself tells me that. See for yourself." George held the paper to Linda's face.

"If you look long enough, you'll see this is Michael's representation of an optical illusion, a house whose soul is show. What he means, is not Darren, but his store of cruelty must be destroyed."

"How do you read all that out of Michael's delusions?" Linda looked down the road. The bus approached. She handed the books back to George in exchange for the note. With gloved hands, she folded it neatly and slipped it into her pocket.

George motioned for Linda to sit beside the window, and slid in beside her. She saw why he made a good friend to her brother. "Where exactly are we going?" she asked. "Do you have any idea?"

George nodded his head, and then opened the book on the top of his pile.

"What are you reading?" Linda stretched her neck and read the titles on the book spines: *Fear and Loathing in Las Vegas, The Electric Kool-Aid Acid Test, Catch 22, Cat's Cradle, The Medium is the Message.*

"If you really need to know, by reading these works, I am making myself familiar with the western psyche." George looked at Linda like a mime pausing for effect. "So that I might prepare myself to live among its peoples."

Linda's cheeks grew warm. Though she would have been more comfortable looking the other way, she held his gaze. Was he for real, having fun at her expense? His expression touched her.

"The volume I have presently cracked open is *Gravity's Rainbow*, and judging by the four hundred pages I have so far digested, the heaviest reading of the lot is guaranteed to bring new perspective." George lifted the book slowly, demonstrating its weight. "If I should become lost in an alternate universe, be so kind as to inform me when the bus approaches Osborne Village. I have business to take care of." He placed the book on his lap and leafed through its pages.

Linda smiled. If Michael were to confide in anyone, this would be the guy.

twelve

George wanted to stop at a second-hand bookstore before they began their search. He walked methodically up and down the rows of shelves, his pointer finger a guide to reading book titles. Linda followed along beside, studying him.

George spoke to the books on the shelves in his native language, as though he expected one to respond, that in only a matter of time he'd find one that would. After an exhaustive search, he snatched a skinny paperback from the shelf beside the till and walked toward the elderly man sitting behind the counter. George, claiming not to have the thirty-five cents to pay for it, asked if he would keep it for him. The man put the book in a bag and handed it to Linda.

The two caught another bus and got off downtown. Linda followed George down Garry Street. He stopped at a restaurant, and held its door open for Linda.

"Are you saying we'll find Michael in here?"

George looked at her with a soft expression. "I am not saying we'll find him at Mitzi's, but we may absorb his vibrations here." George lifted a hand toward the open entrance.

Linda narrowed her eyes. She had no clue what he was getting at, but his kind persuasion won. She walked inside and watched for him to make the next move.

"A table for two," he said to a waitress passing by, though she hadn't asked.

"Sure. Anywhere you like. You brought your girlfriend?"

"Yes." George put his arm around Linda's waist, and escorted her to a booth.

George slipped onto the bench across from Linda. "The most humble of heroes need sustenance. I will order the same meals I did for myself and your brother the day we followed you and Darren in the downtown."

Linda shuddered.

George picked up an over-sized menu and hid behind it. "Forgive yourself. Darren keeps more than Michael hostage." He folded it, placed it down, and leaned forward. "Sometimes you live the life you're given. There's no one to blame. Certainly not Michael."

Linda left for the washroom. She returned to the booth with eyes wet and raw. Chicken strips and fries in two baskets sat waiting on the table.

"Excuse me for plundering into my meal before your return." George leaned to the side and held out a bottle of ketchup. "You don't now how much you and your brother are the same person. This won't be easy. You should eat."

The image she painted on the canvas transfixed itself in his dream. A face that fought with the one she was born with.

He woke startled. Pain stabbed his shoulders and travelled to his breastbone. But, as abruptly as it came, it stopped. His eyes refused to focus. Francine lay by his side, her back turned to him. The soft sounds of her sleep calmed him. His hand slid down the length of her hair and between her shoulder blades. He moved up against her and leaned his head on her shoulder. She turned to face him and he closed his eyes.

She whispered at him to open them. Her fingertips touched his chin. He would love her with his eyes closed.

A white light seared through his lids. He squeezed them tight, and tighter still, but they flew open against his will. An apparition of the Francine he married stood at the foot of the bed. She wore the same nightgown she did the night of the fire. Black scorches slashed through it.

She told him he had a choice. He could leave if he wanted. But he could return to the Francine in bed, love her. He covered his face with his hands. His lovely bride disappeared behind a wisp of smoke. Everything turned grey.

He woke on a hospital gurney, the Francine from after the fire looking down at him.

~

A creepy feeling brushed against Michael's mind. His medications were wearing thin. He hadn't swallowed a pill for days. Or maybe longer? He felt the eyes of the clerk behind him. They weren't the eyes of the enemy. He was safe here. Holding up the album, Michael read every word on its covers, front and back. He slipped it into the rack and pulled out the next in line. Did the same with that, and the next, until he'd gone through the entire section.

Paranoia was a given out on the sidewalk. There, the eyes stalked him, hid around corners, and gave no clues who they belonged to. He was a runaway, and someone had to be looking for him.

He couldn't stay in one store for long. The clerks got suspicious and expected him to buy something. Since this was his second time here, they might remember him. He headed outside, on toward the next warm place.

Mostly women's clothing stores lined Portage Avenue. He began walking the stretch to Dominion News, not sure he'd be welcome again. Less than a block later, eyes disembodied themselves from the people passing by and flapped around in their sockets like frantic birds returning to nest.

Every eye turned the colour of Darren's. The shade of grey just before darkness falls. They spoke to him, closing and opening their lids like mouths, taunting in Darren's voice.

One pair suctioned itself to the back of Michael's head and bore into his skull. This extra set of eyes saw what he couldn't. He punched the back of his head to stop them from implanting themselves.

The eyes insisted he set fire to his family, set them free through a transformation from matter to gas. From part to whole. He ran to within a few feet of Dominion News, steps away from the next safety zone.

The clerk barely looked up from the magazine opened on the counter in front of him. Michael pretended to browse for something to read. After some time, the clerk closed the magazine and turned it over. He took one last look at the back cover and tossed it in a box on the floor behind him. His focus transferred to Michael.

"Something I can help you find?" The clerk walked out from behind the counter, approached Michael with lazy steps.

"I'm looking for the latest *Rolling Stone*."

"You're standing right next to it." The clerk tilted his head. "Haven't I seen you before?"

"I was here yesterday. I'll leave if you want me to."

"I saw you yesterday? Nah. There's more to it than that." The clerk looked around the room, and then at Michael. "Now I remember. The hat you're wearing threw me off. Someone with Edgar Winter hair was in here looking for you. Showed me a picture. I'm sure it was you."

"I gotta go now. Thanks for the tip."

"No wait." The clerk stood in front of the glass door, blocking the exit. "You look like a nice kid. If you're in some kind of trouble, you should get help."

"You're right." Michael squeezed by the clerk. He ran outside and across the boulevard to the other side of Portage Avenue without checking for traffic. Horns honked in faraway sounds.

~

A demonic guitar lick ripped into Michael's heart. He ran down Portage toward Main, his feet losing traction on the bumpy ice patches glued to the sidewalk; he lurched, but regained balance with arms reaching wing-like. Two others shared the long stretch, an elderly woman in fur, and a man in a business coat. He gave wide berth to both.

Michael had no idea where he was running to, only that he was running from something. In one flash, a body slammed his flat and trapped him, scraping his face into the deformed surface of the frozen concrete. The air shot out of his lungs and the weight holding him sent his thoughts spiraling.

Michael closed his eyes and time stopped. An image of Linda seeped in, her expression helpless. He may have heard her call his name. A circle of steel grabbed one wrist, then bound both behind his back.

His words slit through fear and called to Linda. A brick wall echoed back his pleas. Like a radio suddenly snapped on, an answer came from the front seat of a car. A man's voice said calm down, nobody wants to hurt you, we're on the way to the hospital, and people will take care of you. He sounded like a broadcaster. Steady and detached.

Michael held his breath, let go, held it again. He was caged in the back seat of a cruiser and had to convince the cop with the cap on his head he was sane. "You can take me home."

He turned to Michael. "We'll let the doctors decide that son."

"Who told you where to find me?" Michael slumped like a rag doll.

"It's good you've decided to be reasonable. Look, we spoke to your mom. She'll meet us there. I understand your father is a patient."

Michael looked out the window and let his eyeballs roll up. Black ate the words in his head.

~

Darren asked about a Mr. Ballantine at the visitor information desk.

The silver-blue haired clerk slid her glasses up to her eyes. "Were you looking for a James or a Michael?" She picked up a pile of papers, leafed through them, and mirrored Darren's smile.

"Either one," he said. "Both."

"Well heaven knows I'm sure they'll appreciate your visit."

Darren headed straight to Michael's room and took the chance he'd find him alone. After he finished him off, Linda would pay. He saw her coming back squirming. She got off on the drama. He'd wipe away her tears and destroy her again.

Darren stood at the doorway, a single bed in the room. Michael's back was turned to him. He lay facing the window, his knees curled up to his chest. Under a thin cover, he was as still as death. Darren padded across the floor and leaned his legs against the side of the bed. He placed his hand on Michael's shoulder, held it there a few minutes, and watched his chest move in and out. Michael's eyelids flickered open, and then closed. Darren pulled the privacy curtain around the bed. He rubbed his pointer fingers against the lids of Michael's eyes, and pressed in hard.

A moan escaped Michael's lips. His head jerked. Darren yanked his head with a fistful of his hair. He leaned over to hold his mouth just over Michael's ear.

"You want this. Ask for it."

A sliver of Michael's iris showed itself.

Darren snapped the bed sheet to the floor, rolled Michael on his stomach, and climbed on the bed. Tearing open Michael's gown revealed his bare back. Darren straddled him and slapped both hands down hard. He bent low to bury his head beside Michael's.

"This is what you get faggot. I'll make you bleed, and you won't tell. Our love is between us."

Michael's whimper dissipated in the density of the mattress.

"That's the answer I want." Darren kissed the back of Michael's head and crawled down to lay beside him. He wrapped his arm over Michael. "You know I need you as much as you need me."

Darren smoothed down the back flaps of Michael's blood-streaked gown. "Love you more than Linda, but nothing to keep me from having you both."

thirteen

Francine and James. Linda circled a continuous loop of blue around the two names written at the top of the white sheet until the pen's tip scratched through. She slid it down the page and wrote Linda and Darren. Another circle around, and the pen stopped where it began. She slid her hand further down, wrote her name again. Let it stand alone. She dropped the pen and pad and pushed them along the spread away from herself. The pen rolled off the bed and fell to the hardwood. She lay back and looked at the ceiling.

She imagined Darren knocking gently on the door, and tiptoeing across the room to her side. He would sit beside her and say things she wanted to hear.

"You can't be here. My parents can't know about us. Michael can't know."

"They're at the hospital and I'll be outta here before your mom gets back." Darren would draw her near with his hand at her shoulder.

She imagined herself pulling away. "I can't."

He would kiss her and say, "I'm not quitting you."

The sound of the bedroom door closing behind him could be heard only in her mind. She covered her ears to quiet the front door's thud, none of it real.

Pitiful sounds came out. Short breaths allowed in little air. She sat up against the headboard and moved to dangle her legs over the bed's edge. Looked at her face in the dresser mirror across from her. Black mascara smudges streaked down her cheeks like mud. She headed to the washroom to wipe them off, and then to the kitchen to make supper.

~

What they called his paranoia was a real threat. But Michael played their game for weeks and won his street clothes back. Though his discharge from the psych ward wouldn't be for a while, he could easily walk out of the place anytime. He prepared for this, ditched the pills, and stored an imaginary map of the hallways and stairwells in his head. An escape route.

Sunday morning slapped him awake. The ringing in his ears forced him to choose. Having real shoes on his feet made him brave. Michael took the stairs from the fifth floor to ground level.

An empty bus stopped for him on the street in front of the hospital. The driver barely grunted as he boarded. Michael trudged down the aisle to the back seats, the wheels' suspension moving under him like a fairground ride. He sat on the bench at the end and slid toward the window. Forehead pressed against the glass, he watched slush splatter from the side of the bus to the snow banks. A few stops later, Michael became aware of his mind going over a plan. Step by step, and back to the beginning.

His waking thoughts entered a dream that went on for a long time before his eyes snapped into focus. He reached up to pull the cord that rang the bell. Swinging the back gate open, he stepped down and waited for the door, not knowing where he was getting off.

Michael stood on the sidewalk beside the stop, and looked in all directions, uncertain which to take. The shiny stone mosaic facade of the one-story building across the road seemed familiar. He took some steps toward it, changed his mind, and headed in the opposite direction.

He ran along a grassy boulevard beside the sidewalk, passing one bay after another, looking for the sign that said Creekwater. A voice told Michael he was a few steps away. He stopped to catch his breath - a short walk down the bay and he'd be there.

He pressed his finger on the doorbell and waited, but no one came. As he raised his fist to knock, the door opened.

A woman in a print dress looked him up and down and nodded. "Yes." She fluttered her hand at him and he stepped onto a braided floor mat. Her hand went up like a stop sign. "You have changed, but still I remember you."

Michael planted his feet together and shoved his hands in his jacket pockets.

"I presume you're here to speak with Darren. I'll call him." Her stockinged feet scurried off.

Angry words made their way from down the hall. A long silence followed. Darren appeared in an unbuttoned plaid shirt, defiance in his eyes.

He walked within inches of Michael, and breathed hard on his face. "The circus gave you the day off?"

Michael closed his eyes. A vise-like grip clenched his crotch. He bit his lip and held in a cry of pain.

Darren's hand slid up to stroke Michael's chest. "Still love you."

Michael grabbed Darren's wrist and threw his arm back. "I'm here about the lighter."

Linda wrapped her arms around her mother. "Don't cry. We'll find him. We always do."

Her father paced back and forth. His eyes grew wild and he yelled into the phone, "What the hell are you going to do about it?" The receiver smashed to the floor, the coiled cord attached to it springing up and down before stopping dead.

He grabbed the phone and dialed again. Spoke in a honey-coated hush. "You've got to be here in case Michael shows up." He placed the receiver in its cradle and his real voice returned. "We're going to the police."

He tore his coat from the closet, snatched the car keys from the counter, and stormed out the front door. Left it open to the wind. Linda helped her mother into her coat and put her boots in front of her. "Let's go. Dad's waiting on the driveway."

Linda led her to the passenger seat, and stepped to the back door. Before she had it closed, the car was in gear. As the car backed down the driveway, Linda opened the door wide to slam it shut. She leaned forward and clutched onto the front seat. The car fishtailed along the road, slowed, rolled through the stop sign at its end, and sped off.

Linda sat back and looked out the window to the uncomplicated sky. Except for a vague feeling Darren had something to do with it, she had no idea why Michael would walk out of the hospital. Or where he could be.

Her mother said nothing on the way and looked up only when the car pulled into the parking stall. The limestone building on the other side of the street looked like an elementary school without the children. A sign in the yard said District Six.

Her mother reached out to her father's shoulder, and then pulled back. She opened her mouth as though to say something.

He swung open the door and froze. "We have to do this." He turned toward Linda. "Let's go."

The three walked in a row down the sidewalk leading to the entrance. Linda imagined her father's fist pounding against the massive wood of the station doors, having them opened a crack and slammed in his face.

He stepped up, grabbed the handle, and held open the door. Linda waited for her mother, and then followed behind. As they stood together on the mat inside, her father moved toward the sliding window of the office booth. Behind it, an officer sat quietly, his head buried in some papers.

Her father coughed as though to get his attention. The officer looked up, and her father crossed his arms across his chest. "We're here to file a missing persons report."

The window slid open. "What's that you say?"

"My son left the psychiatric ward of Mercy Hospital sometime early this morning."

The phone rang. The officer picked it up and put his hand over the receiver. He looked up and said, "I'll be right with you."

Linda pulled her mother toward the window. The officer hung up, shuffled the papers in front of himself off to the side, and lifted a pointer finger as if to say one minute. He walked to a filing cabinet behind him, and pulled a single sheet of paper from a drawer. The phone rang again.

Her father cursed under his breath. He turned his back to the window and looked up to the ceiling. Her mother reached out, but he pushed her hand away.

Linda felt a cold in her bones. Shivers progressed to shakes. She walked toward the wood benches against the wall and sat down. Her head hung low, and her gloved hands held tight to her legs.

Her mother joined her and put her arm around her shoulder. "Sweetie."

Linda couldn't bring herself to make eye contact with her. She looked to her father instead. He shook his head back and forth.

The officer poked his head out from behind the steel door beside the sliding window. "You can come in here."

～

Darren laughed. "Don't know what you're talking about. I don't have a lighter for you." He rubbed his chest and cocked his head from one side to the other. "Hey. Didn't we have a deal?"

Michael's voice squeaked. "The deal is off. I want to know about the lighter."

Darren squeezed Michael's shoulder hard. "All these years and you wanna break your promise. Did the crazies in your head tell you to do this?"

"Give me the truth." Michael put his hand around Darren's wrist and removed his arm from his shoulder.

Darren reached for the doorknob. "Get out."

"Tell me or something will happen." Michael lowered his voice. "You have to trust me."

Darren's mother appeared from the kitchen and glared at Darren. "What is going on? Invite your friend in or have him go."

"I borrowed something of his when we were kids and now he wants it. Maybe it's in my room." Darren took Michael's hand in his and led him down the hall.

Darren nodded to the bed. "Sit down and let me look." He sneered.

Michael shook his head and looked to the floor.

"You thought I brought you here for free? You want the lighter, do something for me." Darren pushed Michael toward the bed. One of Darren's hands gripped itself behind Michael's head, and the other clamped itself over his mouth.

Michael's head spun. The voice in his head spoke. "Fight."

Michael violently shook himself loose, and pushed Darren hard.

Darren stumbled backward and reached for the closet doorframe behind him.

~

The officer set down two steel-legged chairs in the hall and held open the interrogation room door. James entered first, followed by Linda and Francine. The three stood in a corner as the chairs were hoisted into the room. Along with two already there, the officer arranged them around a small rectangular table.

James slammed into his chair like it was his enemy. Francine lowered herself slowly into hers. Linda took the empty chair next to the officer.

The officer lifted the papers with two hands. "Before we get started I recommend someone be waiting at home. Chances are your boy will show up before we have this file completed."

James leaned forward and placed both hands on the table. "That's been taken care of. Can we get started?" He threw himself back.

The officer pulled one of the pens from his shirt pocket, handed it, and the top sheet of his paper stack to Francine. "Mom? I'll get you started in on filling out some basic information while I talk to Dad."

"You say your son - Michael? You say he left Mercy without consent?"

James nodded. "Those stupid people can't tell me exactly when. They said they called as soon as they noticed."

The officer looked at Linda and smiled. He turned to James. "Your son is a minor?"

"Yes." James took in a sharp breath and held it tight. "Are we wasting time here? Shouldn't you have a car out looking for him? He's not in his right mind for god's sakes."

"I'll cut to the chase. Kids run for a reason. When we know what that is, we'll have an idea where to start our search." The officer turned to Linda. "What can you tell me about your brother?"

She bent her neck toward her chest. Her lips parted, and then made no movement.

The officer spoke to Linda as though she were on trial. "If there's something we should know, tell us. It could save your brother's life."

Linda's eyes stung with hot tears. They slipped down to drip from her chin. "I'll have to speak with you in private."

James stood up and pounded his fist on the table. "You're not telling this cop anything without telling me first."

～

Darren slid down the length of the closet's frame and landed on the floor. He wrapped his arms around his knees and looked at Michael with squinting eyes. "Let me have you again for old times sake and you get your lighter back."

"I'll prove it to you myself." Michael stepped toward the bureau beside the bed. He yanked open the top drawer and in one swoop threw a stack of neatly folded shirts to the floor.

Darren bolted up and charged at Michael.

Michael withered and fell. He sat dazed for what seemed a long time. Darren pulled him up by the arm and led him to the bed. Michael leaned over on its edge, his head in his hands. Darren sat beside him and put his arm around his shoulder. "Did you really think I'd hurt you?" He stood up, stepped toward the closet, and slid the suit jackets lined in a row off to one side. He turned to Michael. "Let me keep it safe here with me."

Darren unbuttoned the jacket that hung closest to the wall and placed his hand in an inside pocket. He pulled out a small envelope and placed it on the bed. He walked to the dresser, slipped his hand under a second stack of shirts, and pulled out a cardboard jewelry box. He stroked the piece of packing string tied around it like a kitten's head. The box bounced in one hand like he was performing a magic trick. He untied the knot, removed the string, and lifted its lid.

Darren looked inside the box and showed it to Michael. "What the hell?" His eyes got lost, grew dark, and then found their way back to Michael. "Your sister is a bitch."

Michael snatched the envelope from the bed and raced to the door.

~

On the drive home from the station, James insisted Linda sit in the front seat. On the sidewalk beside the road, one unbending tree after another passed by.

James tapped his pointer finger on her shoulder and she turned to face him. He swung his head from Linda to the road and back again. "Tell me what the cop said. What are you hiding?"

She pressed her lips together, and rested her head against the glass.

Francine leaned forward from the back seat and put her hand on Linda's shoulder. "Let her be James. She'll come around." Francine slid back in her seat and said nothing for a long time. "Sweetie? Give us an idea where to start looking."

Linda nodded and turned to the back seat. "Darren. We should start with Darren."

~

Before Michael could get through the door, Darren caught him by the throat. The fingers squeezing his neck made Michael's words come out hoarse. "I'm not messing with you. I don't know what happened to the lighter."

Darren released his hold and stepped back. Michael bent forward, and held his hands around his neck.

Darren paced back and forth. "If my mom has anything to do with this, or my dad, I might as well run." His eyes grew wide. "You're going to help me. It's yours when we find it."

Michael bolted from the room, ran down the hall, and leaped out the front door. Left it wide open. He ran down the street not once looking back to the voice chasing him.

~

Michael's legs moved like gusts of wind. They outran the voice and left it far behind. When he was sure it couldn't catch up to him, he slowed to a walk. A highway cut a line between where he stood and a Kmart sign. He stepped onto it. An angry blue car swerved around him and blared its horn. Michael stopped where he stood and turned himself in a circle, looking for something to guide him. A beam of red glared from up high.

Off to his side a car rolled to a stop, and then another lined up beside it. Michael tried to make sense of the people behind the wheels. A green light shone. Another honk. And another, more pitiful than angry. He walked toward the windshield of the car closest to him and leaned over to take a look.

The woman stared back at him and gestured with her hand. She swung it from side to side as though she meant for him to fly away. She got out of the car and approached him like she was catching a stray cat. Made sounds at him, then took his arm and led him across the highway. He stood a short walk away from the lighted Kmart sign.

He walked through a half empty parking lot toward a long building with the word Mall placed in its center. He found a set of doors under the word, opened one, and went inside. Another set of doors sat a short distance down from the one he entered. Michael headed toward them.

He exited to the outdoors and continued walking, covering his ears against the cold. His boots led him to a driveway, a set of steps, and a door with a bell.

A woman opened the door. She had blonde hair that smelled like bargain brand perfume.

"Michael," she said, "Thank god. Your father was worried to death."

~

Michael woke to his mother's face hovering over his. "Shh. You're okay." She stroked his hair and bent down to kiss his cheek.

Michael didn't know what bed he lay in. He searched his mother's blue eyes for an answer. They said things. Told him he was at home. She'd take care of him. The voice that chased him in the dark wasn't here. But another told him to keep the envelope clutched in his hand under the sheet to himself, said it was a letter Linda wrote to Darren's mother.

He couldn't look away from his mother. He might find forgiveness for who he was. For what was done to him.

She sat beside him on the bed and folded her hands in her lap. He caught glimpses of the rope-like scars encircling her bare arms and wanted to turn away. Bury his face in the pillow.

"Don't send me to that place again. I'll do anything."

"I'll keep you here. No one can take you from me."

~

The full moon shone through the open curtains into Linda's bedroom. She sat on the edge of her bed and held the wick under the fleshy part of her armpit. Rolling her thumb hard across the lighter's ridged wheel, she ignited the flame. Fire dug into her skin and she bit her tongue hard. The smell of burning flesh filled her nose. She counted slowly one two three four, then released her hold. Moved the wick to a piece of skin beside the burn. Rolled her thumb again. Held the flame to the count of ten.

This was only a small piece of the way it would feel. She tried to imagine the horror of an entire body set on fire. Her mother never talked about her pain. Linda would make sure Darren did. He'd know pain, her mother's, her own, her child's.

She gently closed the lid of the black and silver cigarette case and held it with two hands. Ran her pointer finger over its engraved initials. She was meant to do this.

~

Linda stopped in her tracks. Halfway down the long hall, Darren walked ahead. His steps were long and sure. A girl from her world history class stood facing a row of lockers. Long red curls spiraled down her back and jiggled as she fiddled with her combination lock.

Darren stepped up behind the girl and leaned into her. She spun around looking surprised. He put one hand on the girl's shoulder, the other on the small of her back, and slid his feet towards hers. They moved their bodies in sync. Linda was once his dance partner that way.

Darren turned and looked in Linda's direction. She stood still, alone at the far end of the hall. His eyes looked her way as he pressed his lips on the girl's face. With his mouth close to her ear, she looked too. They shared a laugh and walked away arm in arm. Darren put his hand in the back pocket of the girl's jeans, removed it, and waved his fingers good-bye from behind.

The tap on Linda's shoulder startled her. "You snuck up on me." Her words were sharp.

George flicked a curl falling into his eyes. "What troubles you my touchy friend?" He stretched his neck toward the exit at the end of the hall.

Darren held the door for the girl, and she looked back as she passed through. He turned and waved his free hand at Linda.

George gave Linda his sad eyes. "Why do you hurt yourself this way?" He offered his hand, and when she shook her head no, he let it rest by his side. "I'm disconcerted to see you suffer."

A little smile wavered on Linda's face.

George faked a pout. "You find me a curious gentleman?"

The smile spread across her face.

"How is Michael? I'd like to visit with him."

"Michael needs someone to keep him company, besides our mom. I'm skipping class. Walk home with me."

~

The room was without words for a long time. Michael sat on the living room sofa. His flared sweat pants were torn at both knees. Linda and George sat beside each other on the love seat across from him. They made a surreal picture, a princess and her court jester.

George broke the silence. "When will you return to the hallowed halls of learning?"

Michael snapped to. His friend had asked a question. He would answer it. "The halloween-ed halls have always been a scary place for me."

George slapped his knee. "I knew you were in there somewhere." His smile slowly faded. "Seriously speaking of course."

Linda stood. "Why don't we go downstairs? Watch *The Mod Squad*. Meet me there. I'll bring some Cokes and chips." She left for the kitchen.

As they walked down the steps, Michael held tight to the wooden rail. He heard George breathing behind him.

George flipped on the switch at the bottom of the stairs. The lights flashed, flickered, and then broke into a bright white. "Such illuminators, these fluorescent tubes."

Michael looked up to the opaque panels covering the middle section of the ceiling. "Yeah. My dad designed this place." He swung his arm around the room.

"That is an invitation for me to sit, my friend. Won't you join me?" George spun his body in a circle and headed toward a wicker chair across the room. It hung from a chain bolted to the ceiling. He plunked himself in it and used his feet to propel the chair back and forth. "Weeee." George giggled like a girl.

Michael observed his friend's feelings like a scientist. A picture of himself having fun showed itself in his head, but the feeling that went with it stayed submerged.

George planted his feet on the carpet and skidded the chair to a stop. "If you could see your face in a mirror." He looked at Michael with unflinching eyes. "What can I do to help you?"

Michael shuffled his feet and cleared his throat. "Are you and Linda friends? Because…"

The soft sound of Linda's footsteps descending the stairs cut off Michael's sentence. She showed herself and paused like she was waiting for what he might say. Or wanted to steal his thoughts. A bowl of potato chips sat on the tray she carried. Three bottles of Coke lined up neatly beside it. She placed the tray on the glass table between the sofa and the television, turned to the blank screen, and back to Michael. "Why aren't you watching? It's already started." Linda clicked on the dial and sat cross-legged on the carpet.

The screen flashed dark and light, colour and shadow. The electro-particles emitted from the television set blocked Michael's ability to read people's minds. The worst part was that the sounds didn't match the way the mouths moved. Michael watched Linda's eyes send messages to George across the room, but couldn't decipher them.

The credits rolled along to the show's theme song and Linda got up to change the channel. George waved his hand no. "That's enough for me. I've already overindulged, and should be on my way." He rose from the chair and gave it a gentle twirl. "Wish I had one of these." He nodded at Linda, and she followed him up the stairs.

fourteen

Linda sat on her parents' bed. She faced a side table and stared at an olive green phone, hesitating before reaching for its receiver and dialing the number. On the second ring, a woman said hello. Linda waited for the voice to grow annoyed at her silence. Not this time. Only soft breathing answered back. She heard her mother call from downstairs, placed her hand over the mouthpiece, and gently laid down the receiver.

She couldn't go a day without the ritual of this call. The chance that Darren might pick up the phone and speak to her. And she could have her say before he was dead to her. He could know her pain and feel it, mourn the loss of his perfect little girl.

The phone rang moments later. Linda picked it up and spoke like the person she used to be. "Michael is out with my dad."

A long pause passed. "I'm calling to arrange a liaison with you. Would you have an opening today?" Linda wondered whether George exaggerated his accent, his idea of cute.

She felt a smile come on despite her dark mood. "Do we have something to talk about?"

"We will. I'll come get you."

Linda said yes to George, maybe for more than the chance to get out of the house.

She walked down the stairs and to the kitchen, "I'll help you later Mom. I've got somewhere to go." She grabbed her jacket from the hall closest, slipped on her boots, and waited by the front door. After a short while, she sat in the passenger seat of a dark blue Volvo, George at the wheel.

He drove methodically down every cove and bay in the neighbourhood as though he were looking for the address to a place he'd never been. "These wheels are not too shabby to be in the possession of my father. But when I have money it will be spent on a car of a different stripe."

Linda pictured George with a racecar helmet on his head, his curls spilling loose. "Where exactly are you taking me?"

"I shall take you to paradise." He looked at Linda with eyes measuring her reaction. "Or maybe you'd prefer a coffee?"

"I think we should start with coffee."

"Good. I know a place in Osborne Village. It's another world."

The Volvo squeezed into a tight space between two cars parked along the street. George plugged the meters with coins Linda fished out of her bag. He opened the passenger door and she looked up at him. "Follow me beautiful lady."

Linda stood and smoothed her jacket. "Are you from Mars?"

George offered the crook of his elbow. She accepted with a laugh. He led her to a shop with a sign painted high over its door. The Ugly Fish, it said. To either side, two display windows held antique cameras and photos from the forties.

"I like this one." Linda pointed to a framed photo of a young couple walking down a city street. The man smiled at the camera. He wore a silk jacket with a zipper and held a cigarette in his hand. The woman seemed not to know someone was taking her picture. She had dark eyes that looked off to the traffic. Linda turned to George. "Why are we here? This place can't be a restaurant."

"Perhaps not by definition. But I know the people behind these windows. They'll treat us well."

~

The basement fluorescent lights hummed overhead. Finally, he was left alone. Michael sat cross-legged with his hands resting on top of the coffee table. The diary lay hidden in his lap. Tucked inside it was the letter he stole from Darren. Linda had held nothing back from Darren's mother.

You stood by and watched. You let him beat your boy and did nothing.

Michael had read her words too many times now. The blank sheet of paper under his left hand dared him to pick up the blue pen, dig out what screamed under that clutter and lay it out.

He started with all he could remember about Darren's place, made sketches of its rooms, windows, and doors, every possible escape. Michael's hand scribbled for a long time, and then grew cramped. He put down the pen.

The diary placed over his notes, Michael opened it to the page with the top corner folded, a place Linda may have returned to many times. He played back her words.

You're the one who should be dead. She was perfect. An angel. A mother protects her child.

Michael knew the rest by heart. He closed the diary and returned it to his lap. Flipping over the paper, he began with its clean side. The cigarette case was the first clue. He wrote down everything and looked for patterns.

~

His heart was a rock. James wanted the pressure to stop. He left his car in a parkade two blocks from one of the city's best downtown hotels and found her waiting in the lobby, dressed as though she expected to be treated like the lady she wasn't: an expensive lunch, flowers, a gift.

James approached her. He unloosed his coat belt, undid the top buttons, and pulled a jewelry box from his inside pocket. This time he purchased the heart-shaped locket she'd been hinting about. The gift wasn't wrapped. But the store's name was elegantly embedded in the velvet lid.

He put one hand over her eyes. "You look too good to share. Let's order room service."

Dorothy removed the sheer silk scarf from her head, and patted the sides of her hair, checking for strays. "I thought we could eat in the Blue Room. Do a little shopping afterwards."

"I can't risk being seen walking around with you looking like that." James reached for her hand. He placed the box in her palm, and folded her fingers over it.

Dorothy giggled.

James snatched the box. "You can't open it here. The look in your eyes is only for me. I'll check us in. Meet me at room 417."

~

Francine spent close to an hour covering her scars with make-up. She knocked on the door to Michael's room. He'd slept late all last week. Today would be different.

"Sweetie. Remember our deal? You should have a shower."

When no answer came, Francine creaked open the door. Michael lay buried under the covers. She crept up to him and tapped on his shoulder.

He woke with a start and scrambled out from under the covers.

Francine tried to meet his eyes but they were somewhere else. "You promised me you'd come to the art gallery."

Michael shook his head. "I can't. I can't."

Francine put on a stern voice. "You don't have a choice. I'll wait for you in the kitchen."

Francine closed the door behind her and headed downstairs. She prepared three poached eggs and four slices of toast. The shower's spray gurgled overhead. She set two plates across from each other on the kitchen table. Decided to slice oranges and walked to the fridge.

Francine clicked on the radio. The morning show host talked about women's constitutional rights. She was about to change the station, but turned at the sound of Michael's footsteps.

A blue tint smudged under his eyes. His mouth turned down in a scowl. A feeling of love filled her. The face he pulled was typical for a boy his age.

"Come. Sit down and eat." Francine slipped into her chair and slid toward its edge. With elbows propped on the table, she rested her chin in her hands. "I thought we could have lunch downtown after the gallery. What do you say about that?"

Michael nibbled on the edges of a triangle of toast, then placed it on the plate. "I'm really tired."

"I need a change of scenery. Do this for me?"

The morning rush over, traffic was light. Francine entered the parkade, pulled the ticket from the dispenser, and drove up the first ramp. She and Michael walked the stairs to the third level where a skywalk linked the parkade to the clinic. After pulling into a center stall, she turned off the ignition and smiled at Michael. As they walked to the other side, she saw the car between the concrete slats on the next level. There'd be only one reason James would park it here. Her heart sank.

She tried to distract Michael. "Glad you came with me."

They rode the clinic's elevator to street level.

Francine and Michael walked the impressive flight of stairs to the second floor of the gallery. They roamed the quiet space, each without a word. Michael studied the enormous works of art hanging high. Francine watched his face for emotion. She imagined him setting his thoughts free.

⁓

The store specialized in European hats, nothing to do with its display windows. Linda and George sat side by side on a bench shoved against the far wall. The fish painted on the mural behind them stood on its tail. Its lips kissed the ceiling.

A boy about their age served them hot chocolate steaming in mugs. He stood waiting like he was expecting a tip, sighed, and walked away. George moved within inches of Linda and pressed his shoulder against hers.

He reached out for her hand, turned it over, and examined her palm. "What do you want from Darren?"

Linda's neck grew warm. She took her hand back and slid away from George. "What does it matter?"

"I see how he hurts you."

Linda placed her mug between them. "What do you know?"

"I know Darren is one person to me. And someone else to you."

Linda crossed and uncrossed her feet. "Darren won't hurt me again."

"How can you be sure?"

"Give me credit. Is this why we're here?"

George picked up the mug and handed it to her. "No."

The boy came back. He carried a tray of cinnamon rolls and held it in front of George and Linda. "On the house."

Linda looked to George, unsure what to make of the boy's gesture. George took two buns from the tray and balanced them on his lap. "Your turn."

Linda took one. George took another and handed it to her. "Have one now. And another for the road." He looked at the boy. "Tell your mom thanks. And put the chocolate on my tab."

The boy laughed. "Okay Juri."

George lifted the buns in his hands like he had them on a weigh scale. "Maybe we should take these to go. You have a bag for us?"

~

She pulled up the driveway, put the car in park, and turned to Michael. "I couldn't have done this without you."

He wanted to answer. You could have. You're my beautiful mother. But the strange light dancing in front of his face distracted him.

Francine stamped the snow from her boots and hung her coat in the closet. "I love the art gallery."

Michael dropped his boots in the tray, threw down his jacket, and slumped up the stairs. He wanted sleep, the dead kind without dreams. He lay in bed and stared at the light show. Flames of blue and white burst over the ceiling's surface and laughed at him. Eyes formed within them, disappearing as fast as they appeared. When he closed his own, they showed themselves there.

"Let me sleep. I don't know what you want." He folded the pillow over his head.

A thump thump thump pounded in his ear. He bit into the pillow. A vault opened and the enemy approached his bed. Michael lay frozen. Waited for death to speak.

"Sweetie. What is it? Let me help you."

⁓

Particles of dust danced in the wide swath of sun beaming through her bedroom window. Linda unfolded the square of silk wrapped around the case, held it to the light, the black and silver strips glinting, and then laid the case on the bed beside her diary.

The lighter wouldn't come between her and Darren again. No one told her. But she knew. He lit the fire behind her brother's sick mind, her mother's disfigured face, and her father's affair. And she'd use it as a tool for justice, a memorial to her baby girl.

Dear diary,
Darren will know how it feels.

Linda dropped the pen to the bed. She turned the tiny key in its lock and returned the diary to the slat between the headboard and the mattress. The cigarette case went into the bag she carried to school.

Standing at the kitchen entrance, Linda quietly watched her mother at the sink. Her back turned, she squeezed a tin of frozen orange concentrate into a plastic jug and filled it with tap water. Michael sat with his elbows on the table. He picked at the cereal in the bowl in front of him.

Linda's words broke the silence. "You need brown sugar. Let me get it."

Francine turned. "I tried to tell him that." She whisked the orange blob sinking to the bottom of the jug.

Linda walked to the cupboard and reached up to the second shelf. She plunked a decorated tin in front of Michael. "George says hi again."

Michael dug his spoon into his bowl and reached for the sugar. "George is more your friend than mine." A hint of a smile warmed his face.

～

Darren sat up on the edge of the bed and planted his feet on the floor. The rap of her knuckles against his door meant she was about to explode.

What was pissing her off now? Before he had a chance to open the door she'd done it for him. Weird how she closed it behind her. Trapped.

His mother wore an apron tied inside out around her waist. She reached under it, pulled two envelopes from its pocket, and held them up as though she were proving a point. "I need an explanation."

Darren looked at her blankly.

She hissed. "I'm not playing your game. Your father is furious."

A machine gun sprayed bullets inside Darren's chest. When he was six, he wished he had one to shoot at her.

She flapped the envelopes two inches in front of his nose. "There was another and it's gone. What have you done with it?" His mother made a fist with her free hand, pursed her lips, and jerked her head as though she would spit on the floor.

Darren searched his head for clues, looked around the room, but nothing had changed.

Her pointer finger aimed like a dart ready to be thrown. "Sit. I'll refresh your memory."

Darren did as he was told and sat beside her. The envelopes lay in her lap, evidence of his guilt. She removed a folded paper from one and shook it open.

Mr. Amsel,

Here's what I know about Darren.

A pain stabbed between his eyes. "Let me see." He snatched at the paper in her hand. She held tight to it and whisked it in the opposite direction. He looked at the stack waiting on his mother's lap. She covered them with her hands. "What is the meaning of this obscenity?"

Linda. He'd kill her.

~

A haze of cigarette smoke hung at the ceiling beams. Linda looked to the floor. Most of the space was occupied with the feet of people from school, the others from a community club hockey team. Their bodies pressed together like they were dancing in a huddle. Linda sat wedged between two other girls on a big chair shoved against the far wall of the rec room. They leaned over her to talk. The bass pumping from the stereo made it hard to hear what they said.

Bruce's parents were out of town for the weekend and he'd let everyone know. Upstairs and down, a hundred or more people crammed into his house. Linda stuck to the basement. Darren would find his way there.

Two albums and six drinks later, he stepped down the stairs. Linda kept to her chair and watched him snake his way through the room. The music competed with an increasing volume of talking and hollering.

Darren threw fake punches at the guys along the way. They pretended to double over in pain. When he reached a girl with spiky black hair, he stopped, and kissed her on the cheek. Something he said made her throw her head back and laugh. She shook a finger at him. He took the drink from her hand, and she headed in the direction of the makeshift bar.

Darren spun around two times like he was looking for something. Then stopped in place like he'd found it. He stood facing the chair Linda sat in. She watched him from the corner of her eye, smiled at the girl to her left, and then got up and walked a few feet away. A boy in a flannel plaid shirt stood with his back turned to her. She'd never seen him before. He reached to pull something from his shirt pocket, a pack of cigarettes. He slid it open and placed one between his teeth.

Linda tapped him on the shoulder. "Need a light?"

The boy let the cigarette dangle. He looked her up and down. "Light me."

Linda slid the cigarette case from the back pocket of her jeans. She turned her hand so it faced the boy, and showed him how it opened. Empty. She closed it and the lighter on top snapped out. He shut his eyes and leaned toward it.

The flame shot up, orange and mean. The boy opened his eyes and stepped back. "Whoa." He laughed, leaned forward, and stuck the tip of his cigarette into the fire. Took three quick drags. He turned the lit end toward himself like it was something amazing. "I have a feeling you take your work seriously." He looked over her shoulder and back to her, his expression suddenly nervous. "Thanks."

Linda pushed the cigarette case back into her pocket. A pair of hot eyes followed her as she walked back to the chair against the wall. She nudged the girl sitting on the armrest into the seat and balanced herself there. Said something to the girl, cupping her hand to shield her words from the others. The girl squinted her eyes, looked to Darren, and then Linda.

A pair of hands wrapped themselves over Darren's eyes from behind. He pried them off, spun around, and grabbed onto the waist of the spiky-haired girl. Lifted her off the floor and twirled her around. She put her hands on his shoulders and leaned forward. Laughed like she couldn't breathe. He plunked her down and pointed to the bar. Pushed her off in that direction again.

Darren took some steps toward Linda and her heart knocked against her chest. She pressed her toes into the floor. Threw her shoulders as far back as she could.

He shooed the girl in the seat out of the chair and pulled Linda to his lap. Trapped her in his arms. She paddled her feet and wiggled from side to side. He kissed her neck long and hard. Her body became still, molded into his. Darren took back his mouth, and Linda rested her head against his.

Neither said anything for a long time. Darren played with Linda's fingertips. "What are we doing here with all these people? Let me take you for a ride."

Linda felt a wave of cold rise up.

"How can you be shivering? Let's find our jackets." Darren propelled her off his lap, and led her through the crowd and toward the stairs.

Halfway up, he stopped and turned. I'll steal Rooster's keys. We'll get back before he knows we're gone."

~

Mirrors tell it straight. A spooky blue tinged the skin under his eyes. His hair clumped in strings over his ears. Michael looked like one of the freaks that messed with him from the corners of his room. That would change for one night. He headed to the shower.

The water pierced his head like long wet pins. He picked up the bottle of shampoo sitting on the tub's corner, and squeezed some on his hand. Rigid fingers scrubbed his scalp until he was forced to close his eyes at the lather creeping down his face.

Michael secured the over-sized towel around his waist and walked barefoot to his bedroom. Water dripped from his body to the floor. He stood in front of the mirror. Wet hair, so long he'd started parting it down the middle, stuck to the sides of his face.

Every second shirt in his closet was plaid. He chose one with a price tag still attached to its sleeve. A pair of jeans, and he might look like he belonged. At a party he wasn't invited to. And wouldn't be going to if it weren't for his sister.

Michael combed his hair, shook his head, and combed it again. He hadn't gone out for weeks and it was late. His mom would be suspicious and ask questions. He'd tell her he was going to spend time at George's and hoped she wouldn't stay up waiting. Or worse, call.

"I worry about you." Her hand brushed his face. "Are you sure you don't want a ride? It's cold and George lives all the way over on Kinglet."

"I can do this Mom. Don't worry. Love you." As the door closed behind him, Michael paused to take a deep breath. He stepped onto the driveway. The walk to Bruce's would be a mile against a mean wind. He pulled his parka hood over his head and walked toward the highway.

He reached the lights, stopped, and pressed the crossing button. Michael's fingers nagged him, let him know they were close to frozen inside his thin gloves. He shoved his hands in his pockets. Halfway there.

A row of parked cars snaked around the bay. A bass drum beat in his heart. The music that went with it hit his ears five houses away from the party. Michael walked past the three cars on the driveway, hesitated by the front door, and then walked around to the back. Only a screen door with an open window stood between the cold and the crowd of people inside.

A heap of shoes and boots lay in the little square entrance. Two steps led up to a kitchen. Another set led to the basement. Michael held tight to the handrail and stepped down, one boot in front of the other.

Darren shut off the ignition to Rooster's car and threw the keys on the seat. He turned to Linda. "End of the line for this bus. Let's get out."

Linda gave a sloppy smile. "Love to." She leaned across the seat to kiss Darren's cheek, and then slid toward the passenger's door, snatching the keys in her hand.

The cold mixed with the drunken buzz in her head. She stood beside Darren in the drifts surrounding the pit. A layer of snow covered the circle of rocks, a scene from a spooky black and white movie. But this was real. The same secluded piece of land Darren promised would be their heaven looked like a frozen hell.

Darren tramped his way into the clump of trees beyond the pit. He scooped things from the ground, made snapping noises. Came back with his arms loaded with crooked branches. "This'll get us started." He kicked at the snow in the center of the pit and made a clearing. Took his time stacking the branches, and stepped back. The arrangement looked like the skeletal remains of a small forest animal.

Darren swept the snow off two of the pit's biggest rocks. One arm extended a gloved hand toward the rocks. The other went around Linda's waist. "The best place to see the show. Let's get that fire on."

Linda released herself from Darren's arm and sat, the cold cutting through. In minutes, her whole body shook. Darren stood watching like he was holding something back.

He sat down beside her, and put a hand on her leg. "Got a light?"

"You know I do."

"So do something with it."

Linda got up and walked to the pile of branches. She crouched down beside them, and pulled the cigarette case from the back pocket of her jeans. Snapped it open and held the flame high for Darren to see. She looked at him through the translucent glow. For one moment, he looked like the little boy who played beside her in the sandbox. In the next, he was someone else.

Darren assessed her eyes. "You're beautiful in that light. Come here." He patted the rock beside him, swept it some more.

Linda turned her back to him and held the flame to the dry wood for a long time. A stream of smoke curled its way up. One branch caught fire, soon followed by those surrounding it. A crackling broke into the thick silent dark. A sudden orange mass shot up.

Linda slid the case upside down into the back pocket of her jeans, lost her balance, and plunked down into the snow. Crawling on hands and knees, she moved her face close to the fire. The heat stung her skin. The dancing lights mesmerized her.

She snapped to at his hands pressing against her back. "Come sit with me." He crooked his hands under her arms like a lever, and pulled her to a stand. She wobbled back and forth. The cloudy night sky swirled around her.

Darren pulled a flask from inside his jacket pocket, unscrewed the lid, and held it to her lips. "To heat your insides." He pushed her head back with the tilt of the flask. The liquid burned its way down her throat. She coughed and spit out the little left in her mouth.

Two hands rummaged through her jacket pockets. The same hands yanked the jacket off her body. One slid into the front of her pants. The other shoved into the back. Pulled out something slippery and hard. She was lifted from the ground and carried. Shoved into a car.

～

Michael stood alone at the bottom of the flight of stairs. He surveyed the smoky basement. None of the many pairs of eyes acknowledged his presence. A mass of bodies huddled into one rowdy conversation. Rows of people crammed themselves against the concrete walls. Like they needed a place to breathe. Michael tried to pull one voice from the chaos. Understand what was being said. Someone walked his way wearing a face of disbelief and confusion. Bruce. He held two beers in his hands.

"Hey Michael." Bruce pushed one of the beers forward.

Michael looked at the can and shook his head. "I'm here for Linda."

"Cool. She's here." Bruce stuck out his neck and scanned the room. He pointed over the crowd with his chin, "I saw her somewhere over there," and motioned for Michael to follow him.

They reached the far wall. Two girls and a guy sat tangled together in a beat up chair.

Bruce passed one of his beers to the guy. "Hey, have you seen Linda?"

The three looked at each other and burst out laughing like he was a stand-up comic.

Michael observed their expressions the way a cop does when he takes a statement.

One of the girls faked holding her breath, and then spit out, "She took off with Darren."

Bruce turned to Michael and shrugged his shoulders. "Take a look upstairs."

Michael tugged at Bruce's sleeve. "Help me find her. There's more to this story."

Bruce put on a patronizing smile. "Sure."

A cloud of doom settled over Michael's head. He looked up to see it hovering at the naked pipes and electric wires crawling across the ceiling.

Bruce's eyes followed Michael's and his expression clouded over. "I'll come with you." He led the way through the bodies and up the stairs. Gave Michael a tour of every room. No Linda.

"I doubt she's here." Bruce called out. "Anyone seen Linda?"

A greasy haired guy sitting on the sofa stood up. "Yeah. She took off with Darren. He stole my dad's car keys."

Bruce looked like he'd heard some serious news. "That's some crazy shit Rooster."

Michael left the house. Ran, slipping and sliding down the dark icy streets.

~

Linda stopped shivering soon after she passed out. She lay limp, arms and legs spread on the snowy ground. Darren dragged her closer to the dying fire. He drew her legs together, draped her arms across her chest, and threw her jacket over them. He stood over her and studied her face. She looked peaceful. He should let her sleep. And take off. But that would mean implicating Rooster. And his dad's car came in handy.

He could give her what she wanted, a new baby to replace the dead one. But rape seemed more fun with a struggle. A fight she couldn't give him now.

There'd be time to get her back for the letters she sent. His mother lied. She'd intercepted them before his father saw them. But he couldn't be sure Linda would stop harassing him. He'd come up with something to shut her up. He loved her. But he loved Michael more.

Darren hoisted her up and carried her to the car. A stupid smile buttered her face as he plunked her on top of the hood. He propped her up and struggled to get her rubber arms into the sleeves of her jacket. Letting her slip backward onto the windshield, he pulled the zipper to her chin.

He sat her upright in the passenger seat, but she toppled. He slammed the door shut and got into the driver's seat. Like a dad with his kid, he messed her hair.

"Stay warm Baby."

The slamming door's echo vibrated deep inside Linda. Something rumbled under her. Her body was propelled at a fast speed. Her eyes refused to stay open.

A light cut into the dark, and then abandoned her. "You're a disgrace," were the last words she heard before she fell asleep for a long, long time.

~

Michael finished the race at the end of Darren's driveway. He bent over with his hands on his thighs, and gasped for air.

He walked toward the front door and pounded against the wood frame with the side of his fist. Moments later, the porch light flashed on, and the door swung open.

Darren's father stood in bare feet and underwear, his lips an erupting volcano.

A voice warned Michael to turn and run. He ignored it. "I need to talk to Darren. It's about my sister."

The man lunged forward and grabbed Michael by the sleeve. Pulled him inside and slammed the door shut. "Have you lost your mind? Who are you?"

Darren's mother crept up from behind. She gently pried the angry hold off Michael's sleeve and said something in her language.

Darren's father crossed his arms across his chest. His fury dripped away and a look of pity took its place. "This is the boy who sets his house on fire. The boy who loses his mind."

Michael watched the words fall to his feet and shatter. He thought Darren kept their secret. They made a deal.

"Darren's in danger. I need to warn him."

*

They sent him away like a stray dog. He stepped out into the early morning. The sky's black was tinted purple. Michael began the walk home with his eyes fixed on the snowy ruts under his feet.

A lonely taxi sped by as he approached the main road. Michael stepped onto it and saw the highway's lights in the distance, white and yellow, beaming unashamed.

A shadow appeared from those lights. Far down the sidewalk, it walked head down with hands in its pockets. Michael took deep breaths, filling his lungs with courage.

He focused on the figure, willing it to disappear. As it came within feet of him, Michael couldn't deny it came from outside his head. He knew only one person who moved his feet with that swagger.

Darren charged and slammed into Michael, knocking him on the ice.

A hand reached out to help him. He accepted the leather-gloved fingers in his, felt himself being pulled to a stand.

Darren brushed imaginary snow from the front of Michael's jacket. "Ballantine." He looked him up and down, glee bursting from his face. "Things just keep getting better."

They stood face to face without words, a soldier and a war criminal.

Darren smirked and broke the spell. "Spooked?" A wicked laugh pierced the air. "I'm playing you."

"I've been looking for you." Michael stood his ground, accompanied by the time bomb ticking in his chest.

Darren cocked his head and aimed at Michael with an imaginary gun. "Shoot."

Michael looked over Darren's shoulder. No one there. "I've got information." He looked from side to side. "You're in danger."

Darren's laugh came from close to his lips.

fifteen

The front door porch bulb shone weakly in the morning light. Wasn't like his mother to leave it on through the night. Darren slinked around the house to the back door. If he threw a chunk of snow at his sisters' bedroom window, one of them might catch on and let him in. They owed him from last time.

He kicked at the snow bank beside the concrete porch. Chunks of white fell at his feet. As he bent down, the door opened. His mother peeked out. She clutched at the collar of her housecoat. "Get in here quick. Before your father gets up."

Darren tripped on the floor mat at the back entrance. He slapped his hand against the wall to correct his balance.

His mother flicked her fingers hard into the side of his head. "Shhh. Are you looking to be beat?"

Darren shook his head and hung it low. He watched his mother step up into the kitchen, and followed behind. She walked to the table, and stood behind his father with arms wrapped around her middle. He sat in his underwear and knee high socks, hiding behind a magazine, and bouncing his leg up and down like it was irritating him.

He closed the magazine and placed it on the table beside his breakfast. "I have something to say. Please join me."

Darren sat in the chair across from him. He slid his hands between his legs. "Papa. I can explain."

"Did I ask for an explanation? Your mother is first owed an apology."

Disdain dripped from his mother's face. She huffed and put her hands in her housecoat pockets.

His father leaned forward with words hard and cold. "We had a most interesting visitor." His fist hovered just above the table. "Come to warn you of your descent into hell." He opened his hand, and lifted a rigid palm.

"I'm sorry Papa. I don't know what you're talking about." Darren attempted a swallow down a dry throat.

"What business have you with that Ballantine boy? And how is his sister a threat to you?"

"Papa. Let me explain. That's why I couldn't get home on time."

~

Darren left the house three hours later. He slithered along the quiet bay. His ear throbbed from the blow. His father hadn't punched him in the head since he was thirteen. Enough. Someone would pay, and nothing could stop him from visiting Linda.

Her mother answered the door. She was a creature from a horror movie. Like someone threw acid at her. But don't blame him for her ugly face.

"Darren. You're back. What can I do for you?"

"Just checking on Linda. Making sure she's okay."

"Thank-you for bringing her home. I haven't had a chance to talk to her. I thought she'd make more sense if I let her sleep it off."

Darren put on a look of pity and hesitated with parted lips before he spoke. "I have an idea what's making her crazy. You might want to ask her about her do-it-yourself abortion."

The monster's face flashed a wild look, then her eyes got sad wet.

Darren had her where he wanted. "And Michael is good at keeping secrets too. Ask him why he loves boys."

The creature lost two inches.

The man married to it called out. "Who's at the door Fran?"

Darren put his pointer finger to his lips. He nodded his good-bye, turned like a fox, and padded down the driveway.

~

Michael tapped on the bedroom door. "Linda? Can I come in?" He opened it a crack and peeked in. His sister lay motionless on her stomach, face buried in the pillow. He stepped into the room and sat beside her.

Michael wiggled his sister's shoulder. She groaned and moved away from his hand.

"Linda. What happened last night?"

Linda rolled over and faced Michael. "Get out of here." She pulled the sheet over her head.

"I went looking for you, but I was too late."

Linda sobbed. The words came out in a stutter. "How did I get here?"

"Darren dropped you off without your jacket. He told Mom and Dad he found you passed out in Bruce's yard. Dad wanted to kill you."

Linda spoke through the sheet. "Is he home?"

"No. They're both gone."

"What day is it?"

"Sunday." Michael pinched the end of the sheet between his fingers and pulled it down to Linda's chin. "Tell me what you were thinking. I want to help."

~

Michael could make no sense of Linda's words. They flew around the room like mini fighter jets. He jerked his head back and forth trying to follow them.

She sat up and looked at him with pitiful eyes, and reached out for a hug. Michael put his awkward arms around her. She sobbed on his shoulder, soaking his shirt with tears and snot.

This was his beautiful sister. His protector. And he loved her with all his heart. Hard to believe she'd hurt anyone. And harder to stop her from hurting Darren. Michael wished he didn't have to, but kept his cards close.

He loosed Linda's hold, and sat with his hands on his knees. "I got home just after he brought you here. The sleepover at George's didn't work out. You have no idea how loud he snores."

Linda sprayed a giggle his way. "My sweet little brother." Tears gushed out. "How am I going to get out of this mess?"

Michael held back. Maybe she knew he was on to her.

Dear Diary,

Michael should stay out of this. It's like he can read my mind.

~

James followed Dorothy down the dimly lit motel corridor. She stopped at the second last door to the left, turned the key in its lock, and paused. When she opened the door, James stepped past.

A fake oil of two horses grazing nose to nose hung over a queen-sized bed seated at the center of the wall. A brown spread covered it. The same ugly thing he slept under when the house was being built.

That he agreed to meet Dorothy here made his stomach turn. But she wanted to stick close to home so she could get to her dentist's office on time after they were done. He sat on the bed and kicked off his shoes. Dorothy headed to the washroom to powder her nose. She insisted on leaving the door open a crack. The sound of her peeing scratched at his nerves.

She opened the door wide and smiled like he knew what she was thinking. Chances were, he did. She laid her jacket over an upholstered chair, unzipped her skirt, and sat down beside him.

Dorothy wore the heart-shaped locket James gave her. He had an urge to rip it from her neck and hurl it across the room. Instead, he undid the first three buttons of her blouse and stuck a hand inside. The other released the clasp to her bra, sending it sliding down to rest on her stomach. Dorothy threw it to the floor.

Her breath on his face felt hot and sour. He eased her down and tugged her skirt from her hips. Her eyes were puffy and heavy with mascara. He wondered whether she looked at her husband the same way she did at him.

James pressed into her and closed his eyes. He wished she were Francine in the days she allowed him to love her. If he stopped torturing himself with thinking and let his mind go where it wanted, he could have her here now. Dorothy moved her body the way she always did, but James wouldn't participate. This time, the game was his.

He held tight to an image of Francine on the night of a party she threw years ago. The blue dress she wore turned her into a good dream and he wished everyone would leave so he could have her right then. Francine wanted him too. No one's touch felt like hers. Late that night, he had it.

He relived their lovemaking using Dorothy as stand-in. When it was over, James cried out and rolled onto his stomach. He sunk his face in the pillow, panting.

Dorothy hoisted herself against the headboard. She shook his shoulder. "Where are you?" And when he refused a response, shook it again.

James lay as still as a rock. He'd vomit if he had to talk.

"Look. I didn't have to do this. You're the one who insisted we see each other today. And now you're scaring me." Dorothy leaned over and blew into his ear.

He pulled away, sat up on the edge of the bed, and leaned over with his head in his hands. His lungs heaved and pitiful sounds came from deep down. His hands dammed the water pouring from his face. James wished he could make this go away. Make her go away. These were tears he didn't want, and weren't for her to see.

"Oh honey." Dorothy got up on her knees on the mattress, and from behind, put her hands over his shoulders. "What's going on?"

James shook his shoulders free and moved down the bed. She followed behind and rested her chin on his shoulder. "Honey. I know things are hard for you. I understand."

James turned and faced her. "There's not one thing you understand. That's not who you are." The words were out and he couldn't take them back. Didn't want to.

Dorothy plunked herself beside him. She pulled at his arm. "Who am I James? What am I?" Her face grew mean.

James sat up tall and rubbed his hands on the sheets. "You're not being fair." He grabbed for his pants on the floor.

"I'm not fair? What about you?" Dorothy stood and clutched at her blouse. She snatched her clothes from the bed and dressed herself in quick, sharp movements.

"Jesus Dorothy. What did you expect? This isn't a forever thing."

"How can you treat me this way? Poor Francine. Imagine how she'll feel when she finds out about us." Dorothy picked up her jacket from the chair and did up its buttons like they were medals of honour.

James stepped up to within an inch of her face. He looked into her eyes with hate, and turned away. "Francine doesn't deserve me. Don't hurt her. Please don't hurt her." James lifted his hands to his head and held his hair down tight. "If you do, I'll make sure you regret it."

"This is the last time." Dorothy handed James the keys to his car. "Let's go."

~

James kissed Francine good-bye and opened the front door to leave. As he stepped off the porch, a police cruiser pulled up the driveway. James stood in disbelief. He didn't need whatever this was.

Two cops got out of the car and took weighted steps toward him. The one who spoke was so big he looked like he could snap the other in half. James fidgeted with the brief case in his hand. "What can I do for you?"

"James Ballantine?"

"Uh huh."

"Your daughter is Linda Ballantine?"

"Yes."

"We have a matter we need to discuss with her. She at home?"

His first impulse was to say no. What the hell did they need with his daughter? "What's this about?"

The big-bodied cop shifted from one boot to the other. "I think you might want to hear it from her." He nodded his head at the front door and waited for James to make a move.

When he opened the door for the police, Francine stood behind it like she'd been waiting. She wore a poncho over her nightgown and looked for clues in James' eyes.

The big cop took his time sizing up Francine and looked to his partner. "You're Linda's mother?"

Francine let James answer the question.

"The officers are here to speak with Linda." He shrugged his shoulders at her and hoped they wouldn't catch him doing it.

Francine went upstairs and returned with Linda. They stood beside each other. Francine ran her hand up and down Linda's arm.

The smaller cop's deep voice made up for his size. "Linda? You'll be coming to the station with us."

James let his briefcase drop. "She's not going anywhere until I know what this is about."

The deep voice spoke impassively. "You're free to meet us there."

James raised his voice. "Where's your warrant? Are you arresting my daughter?"

"It's here, and yes." The big cop pulled a paper from the inside pocket of his jacket and held it to James' face.

~

Michael came out of his room in time to see two cops escort his sister out the door and into the back seat of their cruiser. James blocked his way when he tried to chase after her. Michael made a dash for the back. James grabbed him by his shirt and trapped him in his arms.

Michael struggled, and then gave up his fight. "Let me go Dad. Just tell me what's going on."

James loosened his grip. "Linda's been charged with assault. She's on the way to the police station."

Michael's face went pale, his body wobbled.

Afraid his son would fall, James propped him up by the elbows. "You stay here and take care of Mom. I'm going to get your sister out as fast as I can." He turned to Francine.

She nodded yes to an agreement they hadn't made.

~

Linda was led to the interrogation room adjacent to the one she'd been in last time. The door was closed behind her and she sat alone for what seemed like hours.

The fluorescent lighting overhead shuddered, threatening to extinguish, then surged into a bright light that made Linda feel she was in a play on a stage.

Finally the door opened and a cop walked in. He was the same man who insisted she had a secret when Michael disappeared. He carried himself like he had one too, pulled a chair up beside her, and held his face inches from hers.

"I hope you know I'm on your side."

The cop pulled back and Linda could breath again. A thousand things went through her mind, but none came forward to speak.

"Assault is a serious charge Linda. And Darren has made a good case against you." He paused like he was waiting for something that would make this go away. "I can't help you if you won't talk."

Linda's thoughts lined up in rows with rifles pointed, but she refused to call fire. "Someone hurt Darren?" She felt her heart drop, and then picked it up. "Is he okay?"

The officer closed in on her again and gave her a you don't really know do you look. "I think you know. You tell me."

He got up and opened the door. "Hey. Somebody get that coffee going. I might be awhile." He closed the door and stood firm.

In the man's silent strength, Linda reclaimed hers. "I want my dad here. And a lawyer. You can't do this." She stood and took steps toward him. "Can you?" She thought she saw him wink.

"Let me see you make a fist." The cop made one and held it up.

Linda held her hand palm up and considered it. She drew her fingers in slowly, squeezed them tight, and raised her hand to her face. "What do you want with my fist?"

The cop laughed. "Look. Let's get real here. That little hand of yours couldn't have caused the damage done to your boyfriend's face. What's really going on?"

~

The room became violently hot. The sweat gushing over his skin provided no relief. Heavy smoke rushed through the crack under the door. Billowed up and made its way to his face. Tried smothering him to death. He thrashed around in bed, unable to shake himself awake. Sounds of one after another window smashed by rocks hurled. Doors chopped open. Boots stomping heavy through the house. Men's voices shouting back and forth. A scream in his ear. Darren called out and bolted upright. Light flowing in from the hall replaced the smoke.

A nightmare more real than his life. He shivered and pulled the covers tight around himself. Looked at the window for clues to the time. Still dark. Maybe the middle of the night. Darren got up and drew open the curtains.

A shadow figure stood on the lawn. Michael in ghost form. It flew across the street and behind a house. Darren snatched a shirt from his closet, a pair of sweat pants from his drawer. He crept through the hall and to the back door. Left it unlocked so he could return undetected.

He ran across the street to the place he was sure the shadow hid. Planned to sneak up and tackle it to the ground. Darren glided along the side of the house and threw himself around the corner. Nothing there. He circled the property twice and looked over the fences to either side. The cold ate his face and hands. He retreated to his house.

That shadow would come again, trip itself up. He'd watch for it from inside.

The colour of the sky changed gradually during the time he stood watching by the window. Dirt blue became grey powder, but nothing showed itself. When Darren was about to give up, a raven swooped from nowhere into a pine across the street, and sat bouncing on a branch. Its dark eyes looked at him through the glass. He wished he could spit on it.

Sounds came from the kitchen, clanking and running water, his mother sifting through cupboards, getting the coffee started. Soon his father would join her. After that, he'd be forced to have his shift at the table. Cream of wheat and stewed prunes. Darren pulled the sheets and blankets tight over his pillows. Walked to the dresser mirror and examined the bruises on the side of his face. They were fading and green at the edges. The person who punched him had nothing to say about them. The cop who took the pictures for evidence that night said only one thing. "You sure a girl hit you?"

"Yeah," he answered with a straight face. "She's crazy with hate."

~

Michael had collected the last piece of evidence he needed at Darren's. He walked the neighbourhood streets for hours and headed home only as the sun came up. Tapping on the back door brought no answer, so he headed to the front. Linda let him in.

She pulled him through fast like she was saving him from death. "What are you doing out there?"

A sharp contrast to the cold, the warmth inside set his body shivering. "I had something to take care of."

"If you expect me to keep your secret, tell me where you were."

The sounds of his parents getting ready for the day came from upstairs.

Linda pointed at his boots. "Take those off, give me your jacket, and go downstairs. I'll cover for you."

From the basement, Michael heard his mother and sister talking in the kitchen, though he couldn't make out their words. He messed his hair, unbuttoned his shirt, and climbed the stairs.

His mother looked surprised to see him. She moved in her chair like she might get up, and then settled back. "Michael. I thought you were in bed."

"I couldn't sleep. I spent the night downstairs."

His mother gave him a puzzled look. She reached for the plate of toast on the table and tilted it in his direction. "You better eat something. Sit with us."

As Michael found his place at the table, the kitchen timer went off, and his mother got up to turn it off. With two hands, she carried a pot from the stove to the sink. The sound of water pouring down the drain felt comforting somehow. Two soft-boiled eggs were spooned onto the plate in front of him. He cut the top from one and dug in.

Their mother served Linda, placed two eggs on his father's plate, and sat in her chair. "Michael. What have you got planned for today? I was thinking…"

His father showed himself at the kitchen entrance and stopped short like he'd just seen something that made no sense. "Michael. Looks like you had a rough night." He sat at the table and lifted the empty mug in front of him. "Some coffee would go good with this toast." He smiled.

Linda slid her chair back. "I'll get it Mom." She reached for the mug and headed for the tin percolator.

When she placed the steaming coffee in front of him, he spoke as though she were the only one in the room. "I don't need to remind you about the appointment with the lawyer this afternoon. I'll pick you up in front of the school at two."

Michael dropped his spoon on the table. "I'd like to be there with you."

His father reached for the sugar bowl, stirred two teaspoons into the mug, and raised it to his lips. "That won't be necessary." He took a careful sip. "You can't miss more school than you already have."

"You don't understand. Let me do this for Linda." Something like trapped moths beat inside his head. "I know things." After the words came out, he realized they sounded desperate.

Linda gave their father a secret look. "Is what Michael knows for real?"

Their father took a long drink of his coffee, placed the mug down carefully, and exchanged a look with their mother. She nodded at him.

"Okay Michael. Maybe you can help us. I expect to see you both at two sharp."

~

Linda sat in the front seat beside their father, Michael, in the back. The ride to the lawyer's office took them down streets he didn't recognize. He looked out the window and studied the passing signs and billboards. They spoke in a hypnotic code.

Things became fuzzy. Dream-like. Until a voice jolted him awake.

"We're here." His father turned to the back seat and looked at him with pity. Michael got out of the car and stood waiting for his father to lead the way.

The lawyer was a woman and wore a pantsuit. The scarf wrapped around her neck was tucked into the front of her blouse. "You've got me," she said, "because my partner was called out for the day." She extended her hand to their father first, then Linda, Michael last.

Her handshake felt like it meant business. Michael knew he could trust her with the facts, the truth. Laura Callahan was her name and he wondered if she had children his age. The four of them sat in her office on upholstered chairs arranged in a group. Laura got up and pulled a tape recorder from the desk behind them. She returned and held it on her lap.

"Linda. I'm going to ask you a series of questions that aren't meant to be an embarrassment to you or your family. But have the potential to be painful. Can we do this?"

Linda seemed to have a hard time making eye contact with the lawyer. Michael wished he could make this all go away.

"Here's what I'll do." Laura pressed the record button. "Consider this a practice round. We'll warm up with some innocuous questions, and when you're feeling more comfortable, we'll get into what we really need to know."

Linda looked to Michael. Their father looked to his watch.

"Tell me about yourself. What's the one thing you love most?" Laura leaned forward.

Linda shrugged her shoulders and smiled. "My family?"

"That's a lovely answer. But other than your family?"

Something drained from her face. "I don't have much anymore."

"Meaning you've lost something? What happened?"

Linda looked at their father like he should answer the question for her.

He did. "Michael. Your sister has been through a lot. She suffered a miscarriage. We thought it best to keep it from you at the time."

Michael got up to wrap his arms around his sister. They held tight to each other, a piece of truth in the open.

Michael returned to his chair. His father's eyes grew red and moist.

The lawyer got up to retrieve a box of tissue and held it out. She kept quiet for a while, and then turned to Linda. "This baby was fathered by your accuser?"

Linda held her head low and nodded.

Michael knew he had to say something. "Now that Linda's been charged with assault, she might change her mind about doing something worse."

The lawyer raised her eyebrows and leaned toward him.

Michael looked to Linda as if to say sorry. "Darren has been our enemy for years. He used me to hurt my family, and then turned to Linda."

Their father became very quiet in his chair.

"The thing is," Michael said, "he holds our secrets." He hesitated. "But there's one I'm not keeping anymore."

Linda scanned the faces in the room and spoke to the lawyer. "I think you need to know my brother has a problem."

The lawyer didn't skip a beat. "Before we get into that, I'd like to hear what you have to say Michael."

"Linda didn't assault Darren. Not yet. But she has plans to kill him."

Their father got out of his chair and stood in front of Michael. "Son, I think we should wait for Linda in the lobby. She and Laura have some work to do."

Michael looked up at the man towering over him. His eyes said how did I end up with a son like this?

His voice was firm. "Let's go."

Michael did as he was told.

~

Linda had to face the lawyer alone.

The next question came. "Any truth in what your brother says?"

"I didn't want to say it in front of him, but Michael and reality don't get along well."

The lawyer pressed the tape recorder's stop button. "Your brother suffers from mental illness?"

"He lives with one foot in his world and the other in ours." Linda looked to the recorder. "Can we finish this interview? I'm ready to answer those questions now. No matter how hard they get."

The lawyer seemed to know something she didn't, but Linda couldn't risk asking what.

Laura pressed the record button. "Let's do it.

The car pulled up the driveway. Michael leaped out before it came to a full stop, and rushed to the front door. Pounded on it furiously.

His mother swung it open. Michael pushed past her, raced upstairs, and into Linda's room. He tore the covers off her bed and threw them to the floor. The mattress bare, the headboard blank, Michael dug for the diary. Not there. He dragged the mattress off its frame, and chucked its supporting boards on top of it.

His mother snuck up from behind. "What are you doing?" She gave him a look like he'd lost his mind, but he couldn't let that stop him.

"Where is it? All the proof is in that diary." His heart pushed to rocket through his skull. "Mom, help me find it before it's too late."

"Let's leave Linda's room. Let's sit in yours and talk about this." His mother put her hand on his arm. It felt like fire.

He whipped himself away from her touch. A no came from deep inside and filled every corner of the room. Michael climbed over the pile beside the bed and scrambled to the desk. He ripped out all the drawers and dumped their contents.

"Where did she hide it?" Michael fell to his knees and curled himself into a ball. He heard his father's voice speak over him. His large hand seared a brand on his back. "We've let this go on long enough. You're coming with me. Get up son."

Michael spoke into the hardwood floor. "All the proof is in that book."

"I can't hear you. Get up and look at me." His father pulled at him.

Michael rose to his knees and made every word loud and clear. "I said the evidence is in her diary. She wants to kill him. We have to stop her."

~

Linda pleaded with Michael. "Please make sense." Her heart sank at the look in his eyes. "What makes you think I want to kill Darren?"

"You said so in your diary. You can't kill Darren. If he has to die, I'll do it for you."

"Diary?" Linda made a decision not to hurt her parents. "What diary?" She pulled a board off the mattress and set it within the bedframe. "And why would you be reading it?"

Michael had love in his voice. "To protect you."

Linda grabbed another board from the pile. "Nothing bad is going to happen. Just help me with this mess."

A look of panic overtook Michael. He dove toward the closet, reached up and swiped everything from its shelf to the floor, ripped all the clothes from their hangers, and threw them down.

Linda screamed, "Stop him Dad."

Michael was dragged out of the bedroom and tackled to the hallway floor.

~

He struggled against his father's weight. "Get off me."

A sharp knee pressed against Michael's back. "Dammit Fran call the police."

"No Dad. No. I can't breathe. Let me go."

"Calm down. Stop fighting me." His father's voice never sounded so real. "Jesus. Stop." The knee pressed in harder.

Michael flailed against its force. He escaped from his father's hold, and raced toward the stairs. His father chased after him out the front door and down the street. Michael ran in socks along the snow-rutted bay. Three houses down, he plunged toward a tall wooden fence in a yard deep with snow. One leg almost over its top, and a hand grabbed onto his shirt collar. He thumped to his back, the wind abandoning his lungs. His father knelt beside him.

Michael spoke in short breaths. "I'm not going there. I'm not crazy."

"I'm taking you back to the house. God we don't have to make a spectacle out here."

Michael allowed himself to be pulled to his feet. "I'll come with you, but I won't let you put me away. Not now. Never."

His father put his arm around his shoulder. "If we don't get out of here, someone will put us both away. Let's go."

~

Michael sat between Linda and his mother on the sofa. He shivered under the two wool blankets wrapped around him. His father paced by the table at the front door.

The phone rang and his father was on it fast. The uh huhs gave Michael no clues as to the conversation's content. His father placed the receiver down and stepped over to the picture window. His eyes shifted back and forth, like he was in a detective show.

A fist pounded on the door. Michael looked to his mother. Her eyes said forgive me as his filled with the pain of betrayal. His father pushed his mother aside and straitjacketed Michael in the blankets.

Michael fought back with all his strength. His face was covered with the corner of a blanket and he was pinned against the sofa. The sound of heavy feet approached. A pair of arms, dense and thick, gripped themselves around him, and lifted him like a baby. He was passed off to another pair, and carried kicking and screaming. A jumble of words followed behind. His mother's cries muffled by the deep voices of men.

Michael was thrown into a coffin and the lid banged shut. Wheels spun under him and he felt himself moving fast. He thumped from where he laid to a surface with a bump in its middle and unraveled himself from the blankets. He pulled himself up by the bars of a cage.

Michael realized his situation, a matchstick striking its ignition strip. The rolling coffin was escorting him to the psych ward graveyard. He'd be drugged into one of the living dead again, and unable to stop his family from burning to death.

~

The suitcase lay open on Michael's bed. Francine was told to pack clothes for his hospital stay, to add personal items that might comfort him. She'd deliver them that afternoon. The personal things gave her trouble. She felt like a thief going through his room again.

Francine began with the desk. She rolled one drawer open. The blueprints he'd been so proud of were hidden under a stash of newspapers. The next drawer was stuffed with half-finished sketches, their beauty haunting. She examined each and placed them in a careful stack. Michael had drawn a series of pictures of everyday household items, each incomplete: the kitchen clock missing an arm, the stovetop without its four coils, and the telephone by the front door minus a rotary dial. She tucked the sketches away, closed the drawer, and moved to the next. She found it empty, but a piece of tape sticking out from the front panel's inside wall caught her eye. Scraping with her fingernail, she pulled it back, and discovered it attached to a small square of paper. She looked at the picture it held in disbelief - an almost perfect replica of the cigarette case she gave James all those years ago. She hadn't seen it since before the fire. Michael drew every detail but its engraved initials. Francine tucked the picture into her pocket. It meant something to him.

She started in on the closet, hoisting boxes from the shelf and placing them on the floor. Lined in a row, they looked like a tattered train. Michael's clutter reflected his thinking. Maybe she should throw it away. First, she'd go through the boxes, sort their contents and place the items in categories. Papers in one pile, magazine articles in another. A lot of expired coupons to get rid of.

From the first box, she pulled an envelope addressed to Darren in Linda's hand. Her fingernail slid along its seal. She withdrew a small, neatly folded piece of paper that looked to be a blank page torn from a notebook.

Dear Diary,

You make me hate myself. I loved you for a long time, but you don't love me back.

Michael found himself sitting at a table in the psych ward's recreation room. An abandoned game of checkers sat in front of him. Off in the corner, a nurse spoke to a girl in hospital issued slippers. They carried on as though he weren't there. Maybe he wasn't.

He smiled inside, remembering the secrets the girl shared with him over the weeks. She smelled like vanilla ice cream and never went a day without her feather earrings. He knew everything about her and wished she could be his friend in the real world again. Lee knew what it was like to not be understood too. Her parents put her in here after she warned them about the threat of nuclear disaster. So maybe a few of her facts were off.

The door opened and George walked in. Michael watched in disbelief as he sat in the chair across from him and moved a checker. "Checkmate," he said, and laughed. "You stand no chance against me."

"No. I don't. But how did you get here?"

George gave him a look of I'll be patient with you. "The same way I have every day for two weeks my friend. Through the door."

Michael looked to the corner. Somehow Lee had slipped away. Only the nurse stayed behind.

"You're back George?" She took some steps toward the door. "Enjoy your visit Michael. See you at dinner."

Michael raised his eyebrows at George. "Did you see Lee?"

George sighed. "Her name is Anne-Marie not Lee."

"Oh, you mean the nurse. No I mean the girl she was with."

"What girl?"

House on Fire

Michael might as well have been alone. "There's proof I'm not crazy. You'll find it my room at home. Will you get if for me?"

sixteen

Another day chained to her room. Linda's court-mandated conditions forced her straight home after school and nowhere unaccompanied by her parents on weekends. The lawyer said she'd get her case moving as fast as possible, but the law never runs. It crawls.

Sometimes Linda wished she'd been the one to bruise Darren's face, not his dad. Her justice would be sophisticated, patient and fitting.

She had long hours to do homework. Read. Think what to say to the judge at the trial. Linda pulled her diary from its new hiding place.

Dear Diary, Judge and Jury,

I want to start from the beginning.

Once I was a normal girl in a normal family. My mom was beautiful, my dad fun, my little brother cute and smart, sensitive to the point of paranoid, but always special.

Then came the fire. Our house burned to a skeleton. In the days after, I heard an inspector tell my dad it started under my brother's bed, but neither of my parents says that out loud. Not to me. Not to Michael. Because it makes no sense. And admitting it would hurt him. They still don't get it. It took me years.

Michael lit the fire, but was coerced by a boy who lived three houses down. I loved the boy. I loved who he pretended to be, but he was damaged. His dad beat him; his mom said cruel things, their idea of love to mistreat him until he was grateful. For a long time, he hid his rage from me. And looked for someone to sic it on. That turned out to be my brother.

More than a house was lost. The fire tried to destroy the family that lived inside. My mom will never be the same. She thinks she's let us down. My dad has a look on his face, like he's ashamed of whom he is, of who we are. My brother spends more time locked in his delusions than he does in the real world.

I thought I could protect Michael and Darren both. I wasn't a good sister and saw the truth almost too late.

I'm looking for justice, innocent and guilty at the same time. Don't make my family pay.

Linda threw her pen. A wisp of blue ink left its mark on the wall.

~

None of it made sense. Michael claimed to have hidden a series of clues, and George was to find them and take them to the police. First he'd have to search his bedroom and how could he get away with that?

He imagined an impossible scene. "Hello Mrs. Ballantine. If you don't mind, I'm here to hang out on my own in your son's room, just for old time's sake. I'll need about an hour to go through this crazy list he gave me. And after I've collected what he's asked me to, I'll save your daughter from destroying her life."

George wished he could stop Linda from getting hurt more than she'd already been, but this wasn't the way. But because he had to follow every lead, he found himself on the Ballantine front porch, hesitating before he rang the bell.

He wished he could take back his finger as it pressed into the plastic diamond shape, turn and run. Hide between their house and the neighbour's, and slink away at the first opportunity. Linda answered the door.

George turned to look at the empty driveway. His gesture invited Linda to do the same. "I offer apologies at my inability to procure the family Volvo, but I do promise you will enjoy my company. Once we get the housekeeping chores done."

Linda's eyes wandered from George to the driveway and back. A light went on in her eyes. "Oh, you're asking to come in."

George nodded apologetically and wished he hadn't made a promise to Michael. He stood, anxious for her instructions.

"What are you waiting for?" He stepped inside and on the mat. Linda reached for his jacket and draped it over the telephone table chair. "What brings you here?"

"This does." George pulled Michael's list from the pocket of his jeans. "Your brother asked me to find some things for him. I was hoping for your help."

"Things?"

"He says he left things behind and asked me to bring them to him." George shuffled his feet. "We start with his room?"

"I don't know. Are you sure you aren't feeding into his delusion?"

"Of that I am not certain. I want to check his story. You'll help me?"

"Show me what you've got." Linda put out her hand.

"I will in time. To be honest, Michael asked me not to. Please give me a tour first. Michael's room?"

Linda shrugged and sighed. "Who will it hurt? Let's go."
George followed Linda up the stairs.

~

Michael slipped out of his room and wandered. The one nurse at the station, her nose stuck in a rainbow of coloured file folders, ignored him as he walked by. He wasn't the only patient in the halls. When the lights went on in the morning, most of them crawled out of their hives.

He divided them into two categories: those looking for someone to sting and those afraid to be stung. The stingers had their anger switches stuck on high. They spoke like it was the last thing they'd say and he was to blame. They scared him. They knew something he didn't. The others reminded him of himself as a child. Lost in panic, and running out of hiding places.

Lee was more moth than hornet. She was delicate, tiny, and hard to pin down. She looked at Michael like the only person to really understand what lived in his head. She was kind and elusive and didn't belong here either, the friend he'd long ago imagined to one day have, but wasn't sure he'd find.

He wanted to spend his morning with her. Find some distraction from the insanity he'd been locked in. She was the part of him who believed in himself. His courage. The one he bounced his plan against.

He spotted her down the hall sitting on a sofa in a corner where visitors were supposed to have a break from their crazy relatives. Wisps of her hair stood on their ends, pulled by an invisible force at the ceiling. She sat with her hands folded and her eyes closed, as though in prayer.

She held herself as still as someone breathing can, a fluid statue, when Michael sat beside her. He waited for her to notice him. Memorized her expression. The curve of her eyelashes said peace.

With open eyes, Lee held her hands in front of her face. She examined them like they were magical and new. "Some people don't have to speak. Their thoughts are that powerful."

"And some people might as well be invisible no matter how much they turn up the volume." Michael hoped Lee liked his attempt to be funny.

Lee stood and turned to Michael. "Let's go for a walk. I want to tell you something."

"You can't tell me here?" Michael's impatience charged his face.

Lee pulled at his arm and dragged him up. "Come on. This is a walking story."

She reached for his hand and held it as they headed down the hall. Michael felt he was escorting an angel. The kind that knows how sad the world can get, but can't go home until her work is done.

Lee squeezed his fingers. "Are you reading my thoughts?"

"Very funny. I can't do that."

"In that case, we'll play by the rules."

~

"I'll show you what your brother gave me." George plopped himself on Michael's bed and let his head sink into the pillow. He held the list toward Linda with an arm outstretched.

She snatched it and read it through. "These clues may be Michael's way of telling a story. But they could take a while to de-code." Linda sat at her brother's desk and smoothed the list on its surface.

George rolled to his side and propped his head on his hand. "Michael is lucky to have you for a sister, but I'm glad you're not mine."

Linda felt numb. Hurt crept up her face. She turned to George. "Why would you say that?"

George whisked himself up and sat up straight on the edge of the bed. "I would want you for my girlfriend."

Linda's cheeks flushed and her words came out scolding. "Can we focus on Michael's list?"

George put on a knowing smile. "You can't blame me for admiring the beauty along the way."

Linda returned to the list, and George patiently waited for her to say something.

"I think I'm getting it. Michael is telling this story from end to beginning." Linda waved George to the desk. He stood over her, and she placed her finger at the top of the list. The first item read 1. *Blueprint of destruction.* "He's warning us, though I don't know about what."

George put his finger on the list's last item. "You're telling me this is the start of Michael's story: 7. *Detailed sketch of a gift misused?*" George took a deep breath. "Let's get this book read." He pulled open the top drawer of Michael's desk, removed its contents, and placed them on the bed.

Linda swiveled to the side of the chair. "I doubt you'll find what Michael intended you to by searching his things. Their meaning is locked inside him. We need to work on his list."

"Suit yourself my fair lady. You do that while I perform this archeological dig. Two heads and all." George went for the next drawer.

～

Lee stopped halfway down the hall and turned to Michael. Her glittering eyes said he should know what she was up to. But he didn't. She let go of his hand and glided ahead of him with soft steps. Michael stood spellbound. She was both a dream a few waking moments beyond his reach, and someone he'd known forever.

"Wait." Michael raced up to Lee and tried to catch her eye. She trotted down the hall like a deer on a mission. He scrambled along. "Where are you taking me?"

As soon as the next words escaped his lips, a heat filled his cheeks. He meant every word. "I'd go anywhere with you."

Lee froze in her tracks, one leg in front of the other, and one hand reaching ahead. She held her pose for a few seconds, let go, and shook her limbs. The giggle that followed was a song.

"I've never known anyone like you," he said, and warmth owned his face again.

"And I've never known anyone with pink cheeks like yours. So cute." Lee sighed. Her lips shaped into a bow. "I'm in love with a guy from a rock and roll band who won't know I exist until he opens his fan mail."

Michael's heart slipped into his stomach. "Oh." He looked away.

Lee crossed her arms and shifted from side to side. "Don't look so glum chum." She reached out and wrapped her arms around him, squeezing hard.

His lungs were two leaking balloons, the air inside making a slow escape. But he hoped she would hold him a long time.

"That's it," she said, letting go. "Your turn now."

Michael's lower lip dropped a notch, and his eyes grew wide. "You want me to..."

Before he finished his sentence, Lee's sparrow laughter filled his ears. "Silly. Tell me who you love."

Michael examined the floor. The green tile's white streaks gave him no clue what to say. He cleared his throat and looked to the ceiling.

"Never mind that for now. Let's rewind." Her expression was kind and gentle. "What brought you here?"

Michael rubbed the back of his neck. "Just the crazy voices in my head."

"What makes you so sure they're crazy? Mine aren't." Lee looked at him with unblinking eyes.

Michael smiled at Lee. "So why are you here?"

"They tricked me." Lee's face became serious and dark.

"Isn't that what everyone says and no one believes?" Michael wished her smile would come back.

"I'm sure you've got the same two kinds of voices. Those on your side and those that want to trick you. Sometimes the second set does a good job impersonating the first." Lee turned and began walking down the hall in the opposite direction.

Michael moved beside her. "Tell me more."

"They made a fool of me."

"I know how that feels. I want to help." Michael put out his hand to touch her shoulder, and then withdrew it.

"I'm going to say only one thing. Learn which voice to trust." Lee paused, then beamed. "You're a good kid Michael. I like you. We should get together again sometime. I mean, in the real world."

Michael trusted her voices more than his own. "Yeah. I'd like that."

~

Francine would complete the self-portrait at this sitting. And not return to it again. Once her easel, paints, and brushes were lined up, she placed a hand-mirror beside the canvas, and compared the two images reflected back to her. One was reality, the other, a monstrous distortion, and tenfold the size of the original.

Both were honest and raw. But each said different things. Her outward face, the one the world judged her by, looked worn and traumatized, and couldn't speak about her gratitude to the life she lived. To the lessons it offered.

The mirror reflected the damage done to her physical body, but not her spirit. She had walked through fire. Alive. The image she'd created on canvas sang of a strength taught to her by that experience.

Francine screwed up her face and stuck out her tongue. A mix of sadness and hope filled her. Her eyes pinched with tears that would fall if she let them. She turned to her brushes. This final session called for release. Abandon. Courage.

Her life wasn't finished yet. Her fight with it was. Whatever happened, whether Michael never lived a stable life, whether Linda stopped her strange obsession with the boy who had no soul, whether James quit disgracing her with his cheap affairs, whether anyone ever saw the beauty she held inside, Francine would live in peace. She'd walk ahead and inhabit her own life.

Brush in hand, she picked up every colour of paint known to fire and smeared it in a bold line across the forehead of her portrait. She lifted the brush, held it tentatively at the top border of the canvas, and then dragged it furiously to the bottom edge.

The brush swept across the canvas in every direction until the paint on its bristles ran out. Francine placed the brush down and sat quietly, allowing random thoughts to come and go without interference. She let out a sigh, and picked up the brush, jabbing it at the innocent smears of paint waiting on the easel, and splattered the portrait's eyes.

~

Linda called his name. Her eyes snapped open. A dream. She lay on her back listening to her heart pounding in her head. George. He stood at the side of the road, waving his arms to warn her. She sped by in a long, blue car. The steering wheel yanked out in her hands, and she looked in the rearview mirror, knowing George was the last person she'd see before she died.

Her heartbeat surrendered and Linda turned to her side. George was a good friend. Had she fallen in love? A sense of confusion flooded her and threatened to overflow. She swam her way to the surface.

She'd need a clear head for the lawyer today.

Michael made a peace treaty with the voices. Dr. Ekwueme said they were a call from inside and he should take charge, find his place, and start by making himself heard.

Michael's parents would come to take him home that afternoon. His suitcase sat packed beside the dresser drawer. Magazines, pencil crayons, pens. Everything his mother brought for him was going back. But the suitcase held more. Lee's poem was a piece of her heart. He folded the paper she wrote it on into a tiny square and hid it inside a zippered pocket behind his socks. The words she shared would never leave him.

Three days ago, he asked Lee to meet him in the cafeteria for lunch on this, his last day. He had things he wanted to say before he left: what she meant to him, his gratitude for what she taught him, how she helped him heal, and see himself as worthy.

No one understood what he was going through until she came into his life. The idea that he might not see her again scared him. He stood in front of the tiny washroom's mirror and wondered what Lee saw when she looked at him. Did she see the same thing he did, a guy with questioning eyes?

Michael took his suitcase with him. He slipped into the elevator and waited for the doors to open themselves to the cafeteria. A few orderlies gathered in a conversation off to the side. They laughed as though someone said something they shouldn't, and then left.

He found himself alone among the rows of tables, the only sounds, the clatter of kitchen workers behind the counter. He sat in the same place he and Lee had every time they met here, a table by the window, and looked out to the hospital grounds. A flock of sparrows flit from tree to tree, chasing each other in a dance he tried to decipher.

Michael got lost in his head, wondering whether Lee wanted to be his friend in the real world. He imagined her answers and played them over and over.

He snapped to at the sound of something dropping to the floor in the kitchen. His eyes bounced from the elevator doors to the clock on the wall. Lee was almost an hour late. He left his suitcase and headed to the elevator.

He stood facing his parents as the doors slid apart. His mother's eyes held a mixture of relief and love. She kept her words inside.

His father stepped forward and wrapped his arms around him. He held Michael for a long time before letting go, and then pointed to the suitcase. "That belongs to you son."

"I want to say good-bye to someone first," Michael said.

His father tilted his head as though he were puzzled, but not sure whether to ask. He smiled. "Let's do that."

"You stay here. If you see a girl with flyaway hair, tell her to wait for me."

Michael returned to the psych ward and combed the hallways and rooms. Though he asked everyone he encountered, staff and patients both, no one could help him. Over an hour later, he went back to his parents. They were locked in a serious discussion, and didn't turn to see him get off the elevator. His father's hand reached across the table, asking for his mother's. She folded her hands in her lap and looked down.

Michael approached the table. He sat beside his father. "I can't find Lee. It's like she never existed."

His mother sighed. "I'm sorry Sweetie. Come home with us. We'll find her eventually."

⁓

Darren felt the screams from deep inside himself. He bolted out of bed and rushed to the door. His hand glued to the knob, he woke from the nightmare. He ran his hands down his wet bare chest, shook them at his sides, and turned back to the bed.

Just as he did, another scream shattered like glass in his head. He froze, afraid to be found out. The tortured plea rose and reverberated as it fell. His mother's came out the same way his did.

He intimately knew the sounds that went with the screams: the slap of a hand against the side of his head, the sick thud of his body thrown into the wall. This time, his mother was getting the beating, a routine he thought his father reserved for him.

Shouting followed the steps of his father's brutal dance.

"You wretched bitch. Get up and look me in the eye."

Darren knew she had a choice to make. Do what he said and be punched in the face, or stay on the floor and have her hair ripped from her scalp.

This couldn't be happening, and Darren couldn't stop it without losing his home. He took quiet steps toward his bed and sat on its edge. When did she come to the rescue of his screams? Another hour before the day began for real.

⁓

The air inside the lawyer's office smelled like furniture polish. Linda sat beside her father, the lawyer across from them. Laura Callahan had a puzzled look on her face. "What do you mean?"

"When we were little, Darren told me his dad hit him. Not just sometimes, but every day. He punched him. Whipped him with his belt." Linda turned to her dad. "I'm sorry I didn't tell you." His expression fell away and some of the colour in his eyes faded.

The lawyer poked her pen upside down into the arm of the upholstered chair she sat in. "Look. I'd like to have these charges dropped, turn the tide on Darren. Have him arrested. For what specifically, I'm not sure. At least, we need some new information to prove to the judge this situation doesn't make sense."

Linda watched the pen sink in further and spoke. "I'm not finished." She took a while to get the words out. "There's more about Darren. If I had said something sooner, if I hadn't been stupid, maybe things would be different."

Linda looked at her father. He buzzed with impatience. "What's stopping you? Get it out. Your lawyer would like to save you from a criminal record."

"When we were neighbours, Darren was obsessed with fire. He used to tell me everything." Something stuck hard in her throat and wouldn't let the air past. "Everything."

"And Darren wants revenge because?" Laura waited for Linda to finish the sentence.

Linda avoided her dad's eyes. "I found a lighter in his room." She turned her head away from him. "Yours Dad."

Laura held out her hand. "Let's have it."

"I can't give it to you. Darren took it back." Tears formed in Linda's eyes. Her voice became quiet. "That's not all he stole from me that night."

～

A vase flew toward Darren's head. He ducked, and it crashed into the wall behind him, sending porcelain chips flying. His father's pupils grew small and fierce. His mother covered her mouth with her hand, and backed out of the room.

His father scooped up a book from the coffee table and hurled it. Darren stepped to the side. The book went thud and landed on the floor.

"You would make an illegitimate child? Disgrace my name?" The blood vessels on his father's neck bulged blue and hot.

Darren bowed his head. "Papa. Calm down. Listen." He folded his hands. "Who told you this?"

"You know bloody well who." In a matter of seconds the fury in his father's voice turned from fire to ice. "Your dead child will burn in hell to pay for your sin of buggery."

"Papa. Please. What are you talking about?" Darren took two careful steps toward his father.

"Don't you move." His father turned his back to him. "I can't look at you anymore."

Darren spoke quietly. "Pa. I'm sorry."

"You think I am looking for an apology. My god no." His father shouted at the ceiling. "Lightening should strike you dead so I can breathe again." He turned to face Darren. "I could kill you myself."

～

Since he was a child, Darren knew whom he was inside. His father spit out the word faggot like his mouth was stuffed with shit. He was just as repulsed. His father looked at him like he wished he were never born, like he wished he were dead. Darren made up his mind to give him what he wanted, and knew how to die - fire - the only power that was his.

He wouldn't go alone. His family would be there with him, every one of them. Sleeping. No chance to escape if they woke. Incinerating, not knowing they'd never see him again or themselves in a mirror. The fire he had in mind would accelerate faster than any he set before.

Gas. He had to store as much as possible. Find a hiding place for it. Siphon it from the neighbourhood cars and store it in cans behind Duncanson's shed. The same place he taught Michael how to start fires when they were beginners. The old man had no clue then, and was so decrepit now he might as well be dead too.

This would be a real fire. Darren was serious. Destruction would be his friend, earn him the status he deserved. Faggots don't make this kind of fire.

Pretty boy. His father would never call him that again, or kick him in the ass and tell him to like it that way, mock him in front of his brothers and sisters at the kitchen table, threaten to throw him out on the street. His mother would lose her chance to give him that sickening how can you be a son of mine look.

In the days just before he set it, he'd play at being the good son. Everyone, even he, would die happy. But Linda would feel like a piece of shit. And have to love him forever.

~

Michael's hair was damp with sweat. He threw back the spread and tossed under the sheet. The voices whispered, prodding him gently, not wanting to startle him. Michael, knowing he was awake, mistook them for the tail end of a dream just out of reach of his thoughts. But the whispers grew impatient and insisted he listen.

Michael pulled the sheet close to his chest. His heart took off with skinny legs, like he'd have to catch up to it if he wanted to live. The enemies crawled out from under the bed, and one after another, plunked themselves on top. The last to squeeze out pressed his long cold fingers over Michael's face, making getting air in hard.

Michael sucked in a sharp breath and shook his head until the hand withdrew. He thrashed his arms and kicked his feet frantically. With a united look of disbelief, the enemies retreated to the other end of the bed. He pressed himself against the headboard as they huddled together. Forming a circle, they chattered and argued about how to make him do what they wanted.

"Shut up," Michael hissed. "Go away."

Their eyes trained on him collectively, they answered in unison. "Have we ever lied to you? Do what we say."

"What," Michael dared to return their stares, "do you want from me?"

Their expressions said he was a stupid child. One inched toward Michael, his voice deep and firm, but not unkind. "Run Michael. We want you to run."

A sharp smell flew up Michael's nose and packed itself into his lungs. He leaped out of bed and scrambled to the front door, leaving it open as he ran out of the house. The enemies followed behind, scampering like jittery squirrels. He had no idea where he was leading them, but kept going.

His feet felt like fire pounding into the dry pavement. A smoky blur impeded his vision, refusing to let him see more than a few feet ahead. He used all he had to propel himself more than a mile, and fell to his knees in a patch of grass.

The enemies dragged him up to a stand and pointed to the bedroom window, shades of grey billowing from behind it. Michael looked around for answers. Silence.

The enemies pushed him ahead. "Do something. Save him."

Michael's eyes grew wide and he realized where his running had brought him. The window was Darren's and the smoke escaping from its edges real.

The enemies pulled Michael to a basement window and shouted at him to break the glass.

Michael held up his hands. "How?" He looked around. One of the enemies picked up a rock from the flower garden beside the front door and scurried over.

Michael bent low with the rock in two hands and hurled it toward the window. The shattering glass sounded like psychotic laughter. "What do I do now?"

The smallest of the enemies came forward. Her voice was high and shrill. "Crawl inside."

Michael crouched on the grass in front of the window. Inching his way backwards, his hands sliding in the grass, he put one leg through the jagged hole, and then the other, until they both dangled a few feet above the basement floor. He held himself still, suspended between two possibilities.

"What are you waiting for?" The smallest enemy slapped the side of his head. "Let go and jump in."

Michael squeezed his eyes tight and fell to the concrete. His eyes took time to adjust to the dark. He looked up to the portal he entered in and waited, but not one of the enemies followed him. Cries for help came through the ceiling. A thumping sound, like desperate fists against a wall, threatened to overpower them. Michael got up and found his way to the stairs. He ran up to the closed door at the top. The heat of its knob seared his hand, but he held tight, turned it, and flung the door open.

A blast of heat smacked his face. A thick cloud of grey knifed his eyes. He covered his face with his hands, and let the sounds of shouting and thumping fists lead him. Michael pushed his body along a wall until he came to its end. His feet bumped into a step and he took it. Another wall and he knew where he was. Darren's bedroom would be the first door down this hall. Michael slid along the wall until he reached the bedroom door. Two kicks with his bare feet broke it open. Flames scattered around the room, hiding in the smoke like cowards. Just a few feet in, Michael tripped over Darren's motionless body. He scrambled up, lifted him to a sitting position, and shook him by the shoulders. "We have to get out fast."

Darren eyelids fluttered open. He began to rise, then slumped to the floor. Michael grabbed his wrists and pulled him out of the room into the hall. He used his shoulder against the wall as a guide to find his way. The thumping sound grew quiet and the cries stopped. Michael wanted to scream, but the smoke and heat wouldn't allow it. He dragged Darren along the floor toward the front door.

When he got there, the enemies cheered on the other side. The door was opened a crack, and Michael shoved against it with his back. He pulled Darren down the step and on the grass, stopping halfway down the lawn. The enemies circled around them. Jumping up and down, they yelled at Michael to pull Darren to the house across the road.

They each put their hands under Darren's limp body and helped Michael to lift him. "This way. This way, this way," they said over and over as they crossed the road, their long toenails clicking under them.

Three fire trucks came from nowhere and squealed to a stop. The house exploded into one enormous flame. The enemies clung to each other, lit by its orange glow. Darren stirred and coughed. Michael tried to pull him to a sitting position, but he resisted with flailing arms.

"No. Fuck. No." Darren pushed Michael away and sat up on his own. With his arms wrapped around his knees, he buried his head. "Why fuck?" He drew in a jagged sob. "Why did you pull me out?"

Michael looked to the enemies. They put their fingers to their lips and disappeared. Michael was left alone with Darren.

~

Alone, but surrounded. A crowd of neighbours closed in. They bent down with looks of concern and confusion, their mouths moving without sound.

Michael put his arm around Darren's shoulders and leaned over to wipe away his tears. He looked between the shoulders and legs of people assembled on the street. The fire trucks lined up in front of them. Rigid hoses aimed like cannons blasted the flames. The inferno fought back. Out of control, and winning.

Michael got up on his feet, and Darren followed. He stood beside him, entranced by the fire's intensity. A smirk spread over his face and his eyes lit. Darren slapped through the crowd of people, sending several stumbling, and made a dash for his house. Michael reached out to grab him, but Darren was slippery. Michael chased him, but stopped short. Darren ran ahead until the flames swallowed him. Michael fell to his knees on the concrete. A black force pushed his head into the ground. The enemies reappeared, picked him up, and carried him back to the yard across from the fire. They fanned at his face and smoothed back his hair. Michael felt their long fingers against his scalp, but couldn't move. Darren's name refused to come to the surface. They shushed at him, and said one last thing. They would never return. Michael would never be the same.

~

When Linda heard the charges against her had been officially dropped, she wanted to vomit. When Michael told her a badly scorched cigarette case had been found with Darren's body, she wanted to scream. He was her first love, father to the little girl who had no chance. Images of the good she saw in him as a boy replayed over and over in her mind. She wanted time to stop, rewind, and start new. No one knew better than Michael how impossible that was. Her sweet brother, delusional and supernatural, did all he could to save Darren before the fire took him.

The indifferent sun shone above. Linda and George walked the sloping asphalt path encircling the St. Vital Park duck pond. She rested her head on his shoulder and he kissed the top of her head.

"Let's find a place to sit." George took her hand in his.

A park bench sat waiting ahead. A mother duck in the grass looked their way, and waddled toward the pond. Her brood followed behind. The last of the six, and smallest, pecked at the grass obliviously. As George and Linda drew close, it extended its neck toward his family, and scurried to catch up.

George laughed. "One day, that'll be me."

"You'll be a female mallard?" Linda wished she could smile.

"No silly. I'll have children to love. But, of course, you'll have to help me with that."

Linda took in his words. They made her want to cry. She had nothing to say.

~

The little church was filled beyond capacity. The four of them stood uncertain at the start of the center aisle. To their right, an elderly man and his wife sitting in the last pew turned their heads and looked at them. The man motioned for Michael and Linda to squish in beside them, then urged his wife to slide over. Francine stepped forward and silently took a seat at the end of the next row up. James walked around to take a place at its opposite end.

The minister wore a black collar with a white throat and sat in a wooden chair to the left of the altar. It looked like a poor man's throne. An organ sat opposite on the floor in front of the first pew. The organist played as though she were alone, her eyes closed, her head swaying in time to a melody that seemed to speak to her. Michael sat mesmerized by her composure; by the way she lost herself in a gathering of people weighted by sadness too cruel to say its name.

She played her last note, put her hands neatly on her lap, looked first to the minister, and then to the back of the church. The minister got out of his chair and stood, bowing his head, and folding his hands in a wordless prayer before he stepped down the few steps to face the congregation. Michael wondered what he could say to God on this day.

One coffin after another began its descent down the aisle until a row of seven lined up in front of the altar. The minister suspended his hands over the coffins before reaching up, his palms facing out.

Linda gasped and cried tears that fell hard to her lap. She dug her fingers into the sides of her thighs, bunching the skirt of her silk dress. Michael put his awkward hand on her arm and she became as stiff as stone, a cemetery angel.

The minister's voice began with hushed tones, but intensified until Michael couldn't ignore it. His words said that Darren and his family were going to a place where they would know each other for the first time. A place where they would be a family and have the love they didn't have here. Michael wanted to believe what he said, but a rock scraping the wall inside his stomach made it hard.

Michael knew Linda had loved Darren with all she had. Linda's heart was good. Darren's was damaged until it no longer looked a heart at all. Michael also knew, in some ways, Darren arrived in this world no differently than anyone else here.

Michael dreaded what was to come next, joining in a procession of cars, having to see Darren's coffin lowered into the ground. Saying good-bye to his rapist, to the boy who did everything to destroy his family, but failed and took the lives of his own instead. Michael's heart told him to forgive. Once he understood why, he would.

~

The crowd dispersed and the silence broke after the seven coffins had been simultaneously lowered into their graves. People gathered in groups on the grass, chatting and laughing as though they had been unexpectedly unburdened, as though life would go on forever. James and Francine spoke to their former neighbours, Stella and Evan. They took turns hugging each other. Linda took a walk among the cemetery headstones.

Michael kneeled beside Darren's plot. A wreath of lilies sat lonely on the coffin six feet below. He slipped an envelope out from the inside pocket of his jacket. The letter Linda wrote to Darren's mother said everything that needed to be said. Darren should have it again. Michael pulled out the cigarette case, ignited its lighter, and lit one corner of the envelope. He tilted the scorched stripes at an angle and watched the flame travel up. Half of it consumed, Michael threw the envelope into the pit. He ignited the lighter one last time, and then threw the cigarette case in too. It bounced off the coffin and slid beside it, out of sight. Michael stood and looked into the hole one last time, felt ashamed for what he was thinking, turned, and ran to catch up to his family.

~

Michael and Linda sat across from each other in a booth beside the window. A bright sun beamed through the pane and lit the coffee shop's walls. George walked through the door and down the aisle toward them. Holding books against his chest, he stopped beside their table, stood for a while, and then sat to slide along the upholstered bench toward Linda. His shoulder pressed against hers, and he leaned his head into her hair. She gave him a flustered look and he inched over. Across the table, Michael blushed and lowered his eyes.

"Two is my fortunate number." George said. "I have two books rife with wisdom and two friends with golden hearts."

"Let's see George." Michael stretched out his open palm.

"I planned to order my customary Jolly Mug coffee first, but if you insist, I'll give you a sneak preview."

George slammed a large book on the table. Linda's eyes moved across its title, to George, and back again.

"That's one of the books you brought on the bus ride the day..."

"I am pleased to say I've finished reading *Gravity's Rainbow*, from the first to last word, without skipping any."

"And what did you get out of doing that?" Michael asked.

"I got the meaning to life."

"And, the other one?" Linda looked over his lap to a thin book.

George covered the book beside him with one hand and patted the one on the table with the other. "No leaping ahead, you must hear about my discovery, a gift for Michael. Something I picked up for free from an old seller in a vintage bookstore."

The waitress stepped up to the table. "What can I get you?"

"Refills for my accomplices. For me, coffee, black," George said. "And a round of sprinkle doughnuts." He traced a circle in the air and poked a finger through it.

"Be right back," the waitress said, and walked toward the kitchen's Dutch doors.

Across from Michael, two pairs of eyes made comfortable contact with his. He leaned forward.

George shrugged his shoulders. "Oh, yes. I want to share with you the perspective I gleaned from *Gravity's Rainbow*. I reached the last word, and realized while I knew the meaning of every word before it, I was confused by the story's magnitude. I tried to understand what it wanted to say."

"How many hours did you spend on that?" Linda asked with a voice soft and sweet.

"I took time learning that everything worth living cannot be fully understood." George picked up a skinny book and passed it to Michael. "Now to present you with this."

Michael examined the book's cover. A drawing of an eye, a flame embedded in its pupil lay beneath its title. He turned it over and read the back cover.

George smiled. "I want you to value your gift of voices and visions."

Tray in hand, the waitress approached the table. She placed the plates of doughnuts on the table. "I'll be back with your coffee."

"Sometimes, people have trouble with the story given them." George picked up the doughnut in front of him and bit into it. Multicoloured sprinkles outlined his upper lip. "But sometimes the story has trouble with the people given it."

Michael smiled inside and out. George was weird, but real.

About the Author

Carol Brisebois earned a psychology degree from the University of Manitoba, works with children, raised three of her own, and lives in Winnipeg. Also the author of *Her Sparrow* and *Trip*, she loves losing herself in writing about children and families who face their greatest challenge with heart.